"And are you now?" Avery asked, her light blond eyebrows furrowed.

"Am I what?"

"You know," she said, as if he held the key to some mystery she didn't quite dare talk about. "Happy."

He stopped walking and turned to face her, thinking in silence for a moment, lost in the blue-gray storm clouds in her eyes.

"That's a complicated question, isn't it?"

"Not particularly," she challenged, a twinge of sorrow in her voice.

"Well, then, perhaps it's the answer that's complicated."

"Yes, maybe so, but I still want to know—are you happy, Isaac Meyer?"

In her question, Isaac sensed she was really asking something else—something along the lines of was it possible that she'd ever be happy again?—and he wanted, badly, for her to believe that, yes, she could be. Yes, despite everything that had happened to her, despite all the evil he could assume she'd witnessed, she could indeed find happiness again...

PE
Whe

An Officer and Her Gentleman

Amy Woods

HARLEQUIN® SPECIAL EDITION®

Recycling programs
for this product may
not exist in your area.

ISBN-13: 978-0-373-65953-1

An Officer and Her Gentleman

This edition published by arrangement with Harlequin Books S.A.

For questions and comments about the quality of this book, please contact us at CustomerService@Harlequin.com.

® and TM are trademarks of Harlequin Enterprises Limited or its corporate affiliates. Trademarks indicated with ® are registered in the United States Patent and Trademark Office, the Canadian Intellectual Property Office and in other countries.

Printed in U.S.A.

www.Harlequin.com

Amy Woods took the scenic route to becoming an author. She's been a bookkeeper, a high school English teacher and a claims specialist, but now that she makes up stories for a living, she's never giving it up. She grew up in Austin, Texas, and lives there with her wonderfully goofy, supportive husband and a spoiled rescue dog. Amy can be reached on Facebook, Twitter and her website, amywoodsbooks.com.

Books by Amy Woods

Harlequin Special Edition

Peach Leaf, Texas

His Pregnant Texas Sweetheart
Finding His Lone Star Love
His Texas Forever Family

Visit the Author Profile page
at Harlequin.com for more titles.

For Mason Dixon, US Navy, with love and respect.

And to Renee Senn, LCSW, for her generous help with research. Any errors are mine.

Chapter One

A blast rang out in the still night air, rattling windows and setting off the bark alarm of every canine within a mile radius.

In a small guest room of her younger brother's ranch-style home, Avery Abbott's eyes shot open as she was ripped suddenly from what had passed as sleep for the past few months—a shallow, daydream-like consciousness that really didn't qualify as true rest.

Pulse thumping against her temples, Avery kicked her legs free from tangled sheets and fumbled in the darkness for the baseball bat she kept nearby, cursing when her fingers didn't grasp it immediately. Her nerves had always been her biggest weakness during army basic training. Even the tiniest spark of fear or anxiety could transform her otherwise capable hands into jelly. The slightest hesitation or worry over a possible imperfection had the potential to eradicate months of training in an instant, leaving Avery, who was at the top of her class, one of only a handful of females in a company dominated by males, frozen and utterly useless. It hadn't happened often during her service, but the occasion it did stood out in her memory, far above her many accomplishments.

Seconds, Abbott—her sergeant's voice boomed through her brain as Avery finally gripped solid material and held it poised—*seconds mean the difference between the life and death of your comrades.*

As she made her way from her room into the hallway, through the house and out the front door into a thick darkness punctuated by only a thin sliver of light from the waning crescent moon, her nightmare blended seamlessly with reality.

Her brother's small farmhouse and the old red barn disappeared as Avery stalked the grounds, weapon firm and steady against her side, its material solid and reliable in her grip, searching for the source of the noise that had awoken her and threatened the safety of her fellow soldiers.

When the flashback gripped Avery, it was no longer cool, wheat-colored, late-autumn grass her bare feet plodded through, but the warm desert sand of a country in which she'd served three tours.

She wasn't safe at home in Peach Leaf, Texas, anymore, but a stranger in a foreign land, her vulnerability evident in every accented word she spoke, in her uniform, in the caution she knew flickered behind her eyes each time she faced a potential enemy.

She would be okay, she thought, pacing the too-quiet darkness, so long as she didn't run into any kids.

The women and children were the worst part of combat. You never knew whose thumb they were under, who controlled their futures…who'd robbed them of their innocence, threatened their families if met with anything but obedience, and turned them into soldiers to be sacrificed without a choice.

Regardless of where their loyalties were planted, they were children… It didn't make sense to hold them responsible for their misguided actions.

Avery wanted to bring the many homeless ones back with her when she returned to the US. She had something in common with them. She knew what it was like to be an orphan, to feel alone in the world, unprotected.

Once, before she'd been adopted by a loving couple, the birth parents of her brother, Tommy, Avery, too, had known firsthand what it was to be without a family.

But that was a long time ago, and now she needed to focus on the threat at hand. Still holding her weapon, she used her forearm to brush a strand of long blond hair out of her eyes. When she'd tumbled from bed, she hadn't time to twist her hair into its customary bun. There was only room in her brain for one objective: locate and—if necessary—eradicate the cause of the blast.

She paced silently through the muggy night air, the blanket of darkness hiding any detail so that all she could see were the shapes of unfamiliar objects.

In her mind, it was her first week in Afghanistan, and she was afraid.

Despite extensive predeployment training, nothing could have prepared her for what it would feel like to be hunted. She knew she shouldn't be outside of her bunker alone, but evidently no one else had heard the explosion, and for all she knew her team could be in danger at that very moment.

So First Lieutenant Avery Abbott pressed on through the black night, searching, searching, searching.

Isaac Meyer was humming along to the local country music station when a rear tire blew out just a quarter mile away from home, causing his truck to skid into a ditch on the side of the road.

Only seconds passed before he got it under control and pulled to a stop, but they felt like hours.

"You okay, girl?" he asked his backseat passenger, still trying to deep breathe his way back to a normal heart rate. His palms were shaking and slick with sweat despite feeling like ice, and his brain was still too rattled to discern whether or not he was okay. But he needed to know if his best friend was all right before he made a single move.

He turned and still couldn't see her. Then Jane gave an uncharacteristically high-pitched *woof* from the seat directly behind him, letting Isaac know she was star-tled, but the absence of any cries of pain settled his stomach a little, and a second later her sandpaper tongue swept along his elbow.

Isaac heaved a sigh of relief and unbuckled his seat

belt before getting out of the truck to check on his companion.

As soon as he moved up his seat to let her out, Jane bounded straight into his arms and both dog and human crashed to the ground in a heap.

"I'm so sorry, sweetheart," Isaac said, stroking Janie's coat and feeling her limbs and ribs for any injuries. "I sure am glad you're not hurt."

His statement was conservative. They were *damn lucky* to be okay. After all, it was pitch dark on the gravel country road to his ranch house; even with his bright headlights on, they could have hit just about anything swerving into that ditch. Not to mention they'd have to walk home now, and Isaac was bone tired after a long day on his feet at work. All he wanted was a cold beer and his bed. He could only imagine that Jane, who'd worked just as hard as he had training a new puppy for a recently returned veteran, felt the same.

"All right, girl," Isaac said, attaching Jane's leash to her collar. "Let me just grab my stuff from the truck and we'll head home the old-fashioned way."

He'd only gotten as far as reaching into the cab before Jane erupted into a low growl, followed by loud, staccato warning barks.

A tingle of apprehension fluttered up Isaac's spine and the tiny hairs on the back of his neck stood at attention.

Jane wasn't the sort to cry wolf; she wouldn't give a warning unless she'd seen, heard or smelled something beyond the range of Isaac's senses.

"What is it, girl?" he whispered, turning to peer into

the curtain of trees on the other side of the ditch while reaching under the driver's seat of his truck for the hunting knife he kept there. Jane would have to be his eyes and ears. He couldn't see squat with everything obscured by the thick darkness.

The dog let out another growl and raised her hackles.

Finally, Isaac caught sight of something moving in the blackness. He squinted, trying to see a little better, as a shadowy form emerged from along the tree line. His instinct was to simply shout out a greeting. This was Peach Leaf, after all. The idea of a prowler out on the lonely ranch road leading to his home was almost laughable. But until he got a better look at whatever or whoever was traipsing through the night, he'd be wise to assume the worst.

Suddenly, the figure—almost certainly human, he could now tell—crouched down low and crawled quickly toward the ditch. Jane barked furiously at this new development and tugged at her leash to be set free so she could investigate. But a threat to Isaac was a threat to her, so he called her to his side and patted the truck seat. Jane gave a whimper of protest but obeyed, jumping up into the cab. Isaac quickly rolled down the window an inch and locked the door, pocketing his keys and knife.

He expected more movement from the ditch, but all remained still. Part of him knew it wasn't too bright to follow up on whatever or whomever lay there in the dirt, but he didn't have much of a choice. If he and Jane headed off down the road toward home, whatever it was might follow, and he'd rather deal with it now than have to look over his shoulder on his way back to the house or potentially deal with a break-in later in the night. On the other hand, it could be some runaway kid, lost or potentially hurt, and he wouldn't be able to sleep wondering if he might have been able to help one of his community members.

He realized he'd been standing still while he thought this through, but that settled it, so he grabbed his cell phone from his back pocket and turned on the flashlight app. The low-battery warning flashed across the screen a second later and Isaac cursed under his breath.

He told Jane he'd be right back and climbed up out of their place in the ditch so he could walk along the edge. That way, he'd have the upper hand once he made it to wherever *it* was, and if Jane started barking again, he could run right back to the truck.

He stepped slowly, holding the light out in front of him until he spotted a dark lump, stopping abruptly to get a better look.

"What the—" he murmured, powerless to make sense of what he saw until it moved, which didn't help at all as things only became less clear.

The *thing* was a woman, Isaac realized.

For a full minute, he simply stood there, unable to pick up his suddenly leaden feet. His heart might have kicked up its pace again at the sight of her, if it hadn't already tumbled down into his stomach.

Being the youngest child, and still single, despite the town's many ill-advised attempts to remedy that situation, Isaac had never had anyone to protect. He had Jane, of course, but the spitfire dog who'd landed on his doorstep a few years back, demanding a home, had always done a damn good job of looking out for herself—and now she lived in the lap of luxury, spoiled beyond belief by her human.

But he'd never really experienced that protective instinct, had never known the feeling that another person relied on him for safety.

Until now.

For some reason—as he stared down into that ditch at the pathetically thin, shaking woman curled into a ball there—a fierce burning sensation flooded his insides.

He didn't know who she was, or what in the hell she was doing there, but somehow something outside of him pulled Isaac toward her.

Somehow, he knew she needed him.

When the flashback subsided and Avery finally came to, she had no earthly idea where she was.

This wasn't the first time it had happened.

It wouldn't be the last.

She closed her eyes and pulled in a deep breath, but, as usual, the terrible shaking wouldn't cease. The air around her was humid, and a warm spring breeze rustled through some nearby trees every now and then, but inside Avery was freezing, even as sweat rolled down her arms.

Too-skinny arms, Tommy would say. She was thankful every day that he'd let her live in his house when things had become…too much…but sometimes his constant concern for her—the endless checking up to see if she was okay—was another kind of too much.

"Ma'am?"

The male voice came from somewhere above her head and, within seconds, Avery had uncurled from her position and bolted upright to face its owner.

The last time she'd had an episode, her sister-in-law, Macy, had found Avery in Sylvia's room. That was plenty awkward, especially when the two women had to work out how to explain to Avery's five-year-old niece why her aunt was crouched, armed, in the child's bedroom closet.

That was when her brother insisted they clear the house of anything "dangerous" she might end up wielding in self-defense when one of the flashbacks hit. He didn't know about the baseball bat she kept hidden under her bed in case she needed to protect her family.

"It's not that we don't trust you," Tommy had said in the same sotto voce he used with his children, while refusing to meet her eyes. "We just can't risk anything happening. It's for the best."

Avery's stomach churned at the memory. The worst part was, her brother was absolutely correct. If she'd had anywhere else to go after that, she would have. But she did not. And, worse, she was completely dependent on the few remaining people in her life—the few that hadn't given up on her—for everything.

But that was the last time.

This time, from what little she could deduce in a quick survey of her surroundings, might just turn out to be downright humiliating.

He spoke again. "Is there anything I can do to help you?" he asked. "Are you lost?"

Avery almost grinned at that last part, because yes, indeed, she was very, very lost.

The only thing that stopped her was the tone of the man's voice. Glancing around, she could see that she was completely alone in some dirt hole on the side of a gravel country road, in—she looked down at her body—a thin white tank and army-issue workout shorts. Clearly she was at the mercy of this guy, who'd evidently stopped to check on her. Under other circumstances, her training would have kicked in and she'd have flipped him onto his back in mere seconds.

But something told her he wasn't a threat.

His voice.

It was deep and smooth, his words bathed in the local accent, and full of genuine concern. On top of that, he stood above the ditch staring down at her, hands at his sides, and hadn't made a single move to come closer. The man seemed...*safe*.

Having lost her bat somewhere along the way, she braced herself for an attack when he bent his knees, but instead of jumping into the ditch with her like she thought he might, the man simply knelt down.

The movement brought attention to long, muscled thighs beneath faded denim jeans, and when he leaned an elbow on his upright knee, Avery noticed the stretch of tendons in his sinewy forearms.

How ridiculous it was, she thought, for her to notice such a stupid thing when her life could be in danger for all she knew. Seeing as how the guy hadn't mauled her by now, it probably wasn't, but still—it could be.

Avery crossed her arms over her thinly clad chest. Not that there was much to see there. Not anymore.

"I'm fine, actually. Just…taking a walk. Enjoying the stars and all." She waved a hand above her, indicating the spread of twinkling lights above them. It was plausible.

But when she looked up into his eyes, she could tell he didn't agree. The man looked to be somewhere near her own age, maybe slightly older, and Avery was surprised she'd never seen him before. She'd grown up in Peach Leaf and knew just about everybody, so it was strange that she hadn't met this person.

Sure as hell would remember if she had.

Not only did he have the toned body of someone who either worked at it or had a very active job—he had a face to do it justice. Clear, dark chocolate eyes—eyes that had a certain glint in them, as though they saw more than most—a strong jaw and hair the color of a panther's coat.

Right now those brown eyes narrowed with what appeared to be strong suspicion, but after a few seconds, they filled with a certain kind of warmth Avery wasn't used to seeing anymore.

Pity—she was used to that—but not warmth.

"It is a beautiful night, isn't it?" he said, seeming to relax a little.

There was something easy about him that made Avery want to let her guard down a smidge. It was almost as if his mere presence lowered her blood pressure.

"That it is," she agreed, wanting the strange exchange to be over so she could figure out how far she'd gotten and how, for the love of all things holy, she was supposed to get back home.

"Name's Isaac," the man said, stretching out a large hand.

Even in the dark, Avery could see calluses and healed-over scratches. Must be some kind of laborer.

She just stared at him, not offering her name, willing him to take his leave. It would be futile to try to explain the complexities of her *condition*, as she'd come to think of it, to this handsome stranger. She didn't even completely understand it herself, even after almost a year of therapy. Besides, her knees were beginning to feel a little wobbly and a spot just above her left temple had started to ache...

"Well, if you're all set here—" he looked like he believed her to be anything but "—I've got a walk ahead of me."

Isaac hesitated for a long moment, then nodded and turned to leave.

Avery was about to do the same when everything went blacker than the night sky.

Isaac had just started back toward his truck—every nerve in his body telling him to stay behind—when he heard a thud.

He whipped back around and broke into a run when he saw that the woman had collapsed in a heap, dust billowing around her.

Crap.

He knew he should have stayed put and tried to talk her into letting him help. It didn't take a genius to see she was in some kind of trouble.

Walking even a few yards away from her had gone against his every instinct, but he hadn't planned to actually leave her alone in the middle of the night, not for a single moment. He just needed a second to regroup.

His legs made quick work of the distance that separated them and seconds later he plunged into the ditch and reached her side, lifting the woman's negligible weight into his arms and propping her up so she might draw in deeper breaths. Her skin was clammy and she seemed to flutter on the verge of consciousness as she pulled in shallow doses of air.

Isaac had no idea what steps to take from there; as a certified dog trainer, he was generally better prepared for canine emergencies than those of his own species. His heart beat frantically for several long minutes as he held her, waiting for her to come back so he could better help her. As slow seconds beat past, he studied the woman in his grasp, seeing for the first time how lovely she was.

Her long blond hair seemed to shimmer in the moonlight, its corn-silk strands tickling his arms where it fell. Creamy skin, just a shade or two lighter than her hair, lay like soft linen over sculpted cheekbones, creating a perfect canvas for full lips and large eyes, the color of which he suddenly longed to know.

She wore a white T-shirt and athletic shorts, and Isaac grimaced when he caught sight of the sharp ridge of collarbone peeking out the top of the threadbare cotton. She was so very thin. No wonder lifting her had felt no more difficult than picking up Jane. A glint of metal got his attention and he reached up to search for a pendant attached to a silver chain around her neck, adjusting her so he could remain supporting her with one arm.

Running his finger along the tiny links, Isaac finally touched an ID tag of some sort and pulled it closer to his face.

It was an army-issue dog tag; he'd recognize it anywhere because of his brother, Stephen, and working with so many veterans and their companions at his dog training facility. This one was engraved *A. Abbott.*

Somehow seeing her name made him even more impatient to wake her up. He knew nothing about the pretty woman, except that she looked like she could stand to eat a quarter pounder or two, but something about her pulled him in and wouldn't let go.

His buddies would've teased him relentlessly if they could have seen him then. *Meyer can't resist a damsel in distress*, he could almost hear them say, joshing at his tendency to offer assistance to every granny who chanced to cross a street in Peach Leaf or any single mom who needed the use of his truck for a move.

But this one was different.

Before she'd tumbled to the ground, Isaac had seen enough to know that Abbott was no damsel in distress. Her voice had been tough—commanding, almost—and, despite her smallness, she'd stood tall and carried herself with authority and confidence. It was her body that had finally lost its resolve—no doubt, from the look of things, due to not eating enough—not her mind or her survival instinct.

Now that he'd seen the tag, he understood why.

Now that he'd seen the tag, he'd also begun to form an idea of what might have happened to her and, more important, how he might be able to help.

Chapter Two

Avery woke for the second time that night about an hour later.

For a moment, forgetting the strange dreamlike events of the night, she thought she might be back at home safe in her bed while Tommy and Macy cooked breakfast for her niece and nephew.

But when Avery sat up and opened her eyes, a rush of panic hit her like a bucket of ice water and she shot up from an unfamiliar couch, gasping for breath as she fully realized that she had no idea where she was.

Again.

A hand-knit afghan in alternating tones of light and dark blues tumbled to the floor, covering her feet, and as her eyes adjusted to the golden light coming from a nearby table lamp, Avery glanced briefly around the room. It was minimally decorated but cozy, and she wondered at the comfort it provided despite its newness to her.

"Easy there," a low voice came from behind the sofa and she nearly jumped out of her skin.

Avery put up her fists and turned around in one quick motion, ready to face whatever situation her unpredictable, unreliable mind had gotten her into now.

"Who are you, and where the hell am I?" she spat out, willing her voice to mask the fear that was quickly weaving its way from her gut to her chest.

The nightmares were bad enough, but the flashbacks, rarer though they were, absolutely terrified her. This wasn't the first time she'd found herself in a place from which she couldn't retrace her steps. If it happened on too many more occasions, she didn't even want to think about the action her family and therapist might agree on against her will. She'd already lost her job and her own place. The thought of being locked up somewhere...

The man in front of her gently placed the cell phone he'd been holding on a small end table, immediately holding up both of his hands. She vaguely recalled his handsome face as a tiny slice of memory slipped from the recesses of her mind, but it vanished before she could catch it, leaving her with nothing helpful.

"My name's Isaac. Isaac Meyer. I'm not gonna hurt you. And obviously you don't remember—you were pretty out of it—but we did meet earlier." A Southern accent similar to her own slid over the man's words like hot gravy, identifying him as a local.

"Avery," she murmured.

He stood completely still as Avery looked him up and down, her soldier's instincts and peripheral vision checking every inch of his person, even as her eyes remained steadily locked on to his. They were a rich brown, she noticed, instantly chastising herself for wasting time on such a silly thought when she faced a potential enemy.

When Avery didn't speak for a long moment, he continued.

"Look, I know this has been a strange night, at least for me, but—" He hesitated and seemed to be working through his thoughts before speaking. "I found you on the side of the road. In a ditch. Jane and I didn't know what to do and there wasn't a damn thing could be done to help you out there in the dark, so we brought you back here."

He lowered one hand, slowly and cautiously as if trying not to unsettle a rabid animal, and pointed toward the phone before putting his hand back up. "I was just about to call 9-1-1 and see about getting someone out here to check on you. Then you woke up and, well, here we are."

Avery had no recollection of meeting him earlier, only his word to go on and the vague, déjà vu–like inkling that she'd seen him before. The past few hours were as blank as a fresh sheet of paper. In all he'd said, only one insignificant thing stuck out to her. That seemed the way of it lately. If she couldn't focus on everything, she picked out the smallest bit and used that to ground her in reality. It was one of the few things her therapist had taught her that she'd actually practiced.

"Jane? Who's Jane?" she asked, wondering, of all things, why that particular piece of information mattered.

At the mention of the name, Isaac's features noticeably softened and Avery let her body do likewise, relaxing a little as she checked off facts in her head. One—if he'd a mind to, he could have murdered her already. Two—the man had placed a homemade blanket on her, for goodness' sake. What murderer did such a thing? And three—if he was to be believed, and there was no clear indication why he shouldn't at this point, as she was standing there unharmed in his comfortable home, he'd been about to call for help, something she absolutely did *not* want him to do. Thank goodness she'd woken up in time to prevent that from happening. The very last thing she needed right now was for Tommy or her parents to have another reason to worry about her. Of all the things she hated about her PTSD, perhaps the worst was the way it had turned a grown, successful woman into a child, or at least that's how her family saw her.

She had to get back home as soon as possible, but first, she needed to find out exactly how far her deceitful mind had dragged her this time.

She waited for an answer to her question but instead of providing one, Isaac gave a sharp whistle and a large dog of an unidentifiable breed, with an unruly coat consisting of about a hundred varying shades of brown, strolled into the room to sit beside him, looking up at its human with what could only be described as pure adoration. Man looked down at dog with open pride.

"Avery, meet Jane," he said, then gave the canine some sort of hand signal.

Before she could protest, the dog was standing in front of her. She watched, unmoving, as Jane reached out a large, fuzzy paw and stared expectantly up at her with huge brown eyes. The whole thing was so absurdly cute that Avery couldn't keep a smile from curving at the edge of her lips. Noticing for the first time that she still held her fists defensively in front of her, Avery lowered both hands and reached one out to grasp the offered paw. The warm, soft fur was instantly sooth-ing, but when Jane took back her paw and pressed her large, heavy head against Avery's thighs, her tail break-ing into a slow wag as she waited for her doggie hug to be reciprocated, Avery's heart caught in her throat.

A wave of emotion swept over her like an evening tide and her knees nearly buckled beneath her. She was suddenly, desperately sad. And oh-so-tired. Tired of being dependent on others to keep her safe when she'd once been so self-reliant. Tired of being locked in-side her own head. Tired of being afraid to go to sleep, knowing the nightmares would meet her there like a mugger waiting in the shade of night for his next vic-tim, and tired of feeling crazy when she knew—even if everyone else believed otherwise—that she was not.

She gently pushed the dog away and sat down on the sofa. Jane jumped up, too, but sat a few feet away, as if giving Avery her space. Isaac moved across the room to sit in a chair on the other side of a mahogany coffee table. He folded his hands in his lap and looked at the floor. Avery knew she should keep an eye on him until she could get out of there but her lids felt weighted and she let them slip closed for just a second as she gathered her thoughts.

"How long was I out?" she asked, swallowing, not really wanting to know the answer. Her flashbacks, blackouts, whatever the hell they were, sometimes lasted for hours before she came back around. She hated the loss of control and the resulting feeling of irresponsibility, as though she'd had too much to drink and passed out at the wheel.

She looked up at Isaac, meeting his eyes. In them, she found none of the things she'd expected: pity, irritation, confusion. Instead, they were like deep woods in the middle of the night—quiet, dark, mysterious—but for some reason, she felt safe there. She knew enough to sense menace when it lurked, and so she knew then as sure as she knew her own name and rank that this man was not dangerous.

"About an hour," he said, his voice smooth like strong coffee. "Took me half of that to get you here. My truck broke down just up the road and my cell had almost no charge left. You were pretty cold when Jane and I got you inside the house, so I covered you with a blanket and plugged in the phone for ten minutes or so. You didn't seem wounded or anything, but it's not every day I find people prowling around in the dark, so I figured best thing to do was call the authorities and let them make sure you're okay and sort you out."

Isaac paused, brow furrowed, and it seemed he might say more, but then he closed his mouth and looked at her expectantly.

She sifted through his comments, appreciating his effort and the fact that, other than to carry her, he hadn't handled her any more than necessary; in fact, he seemed wary of being anywhere near her—a thought that touched her heart with the gentlemanliness it bespoke. His simple, strong kindness reminded her of some of the men she'd served alongside, and for a fleeting moment, she missed her comrades.

There had been a time, not that long after returning home, when she would have done anything to forget her tours overseas if it would have helped her blend back in to civilian society. But after being back in Peach Leaf for a few months, newly burdened with the knowledge that such a wish might never come true, she'd begun to long for another deployment, if only for the fact that she didn't know how to be "normal" anymore, whatever that meant. She didn't belong in her own world, and she hadn't truly belonged in that barren, violence-riddled land, so the question was, as always: Where, if anywhere, did she belong?

"You could have left me there, you know," Avery said. "I didn't need any help." The words sounded hollow and impractical even as she spoke them.

"We both know that's not true," he answered, his tone thankfully free of judgment.

She didn't want to have to explain herself to a complete stranger. Even a kind, gentle, admittedly handsome stranger.

"All the same, though," he continued, "I don't think it's safe for you to walk home on your own and, as I said, my truck's out of commission for the night. Is there anyone you can call to—"

"No!" she shouted as her body simultaneously lurched forward a few feet, startling them both. She covered her mouth with her hand, the skin icy against her warm lips.

"Look, if you're in some kind of dicey situation, it ain't any of my business, but I can't let you stay out here alone in the dark, either.

She shook her head and lowered her hand, clasping it between her knees. "No, no, it's not like that. I'm not… I mean… I just have these episodes sometimes, and occasionally I lose track of where I am." She stopped abruptly, not really knowing what else to say but thankfully, he didn't seem to expect much more. Trying to put her problems into words was always a fragile balancing act of saying too little or too much. Even though they appreciated her service, she'd quickly discovered that most people would rather not think or talk about the things that Avery had experienced, and it was hard to describe something she herself didn't fully understand.

Isaac swallowed and held out his hands, palms up. His face was difficult to read but not hardened, and his expression gave her the idea that he was genuinely waiting to hear what she had to say, who she was, before making his mind up about her. It was refreshing. In her small town, Avery was used to people thinking they knew everything about each other just because they'd racked up some years together in the same place. They made the frequent mistake of assuming that you'd always be who you once were.

"Speaking of," she went on, struggling to hide her sudden embarrassment at having to ask, "would you mind telling me where we are?"

Isaac's lids lowered and his mouth relaxed into an easy grin, as if he'd been waiting for her to ask so he could have something helpful to offer. "Sure thing. We're about two miles outside of Peach Leaf proper, and my house is about half a mile from Ranch Road 64. Closest landmark is Dewberry Farms, my neighbor."

His neighbor. Her brother.

Avery released an audible sigh of relief that she hadn't wandered too far from home in her—she looked down, suddenly aware of the goose bumps that had formed a tiny mountain range along her arms—*very* thin pajamas. Thank goodness she'd been unable to shed the habit of sleeping in her sports bra or she'd have been sitting in a stranger's living room without a shred of modesty.

"Dewberry is my home, at least for now," she said, and Isaac nodded, seeming unsurprised. He probably knew her recent history as well as any of the other locals. It said a lot about his character that he wasn't acting as though that meant he knew *her*.

"Well, as you know, it's not far from here. I think I feel well enough to walk back now. If I don't make it home before everyone wakes up, they'll be worried, so—" she pointed a thumb in the general direction of the front door "—I should probably get going."

Isaac held out a hand as she stood. "I don't think that's such a good idea."

"Why not?" She rolled her eyes almost immediately,

sitting back down as the inside of her head did another dizzy spin. "I mean, I know why not, but how is it any of your business? I appreciate you helping me, but I'm okay now."

Isaac shook his head. "For one thing, you're pale as a ghost, and let's not forget you were passed out for a solid hour. Plus, pardon my saying so, but you look like you could use some energy if you're going to walk a half mile, which, for the record, I'd recommend putting off until the sun comes up."

Avery bit her lip, considering. Everything he said was absolutely right, but she couldn't risk letting Tommy or Macy find her bed empty again. She wouldn't put them through that worry another time.

Her brother and sister-in-law had already given her a place to stay and a hell of a lot of support through the lowest point in her life so far, for which she'd never be able to repay them. They said they were glad to do it and they meant well, but Avery wasn't naive, and she wasn't blind; she could see the way they looked at her when they insisted she was no imposition, as if they weren't sure what she might do next, or worse, how her involuntary actions might affect their kids. She could see the way they walked on eggshells around her. The familiar guilt made her empty stomach clench in pain.

She sat back down on the sofa and Jane thumped her tail against the worn fabric. Avery reached over to pet the dog's soft fur, surprised once again at how comforting it was just to stroke Jane's broad back. When she gave Jane a few scratches behind her enormous, fuzzy ears and the scruffy mutt closed her eyes in bliss, Avery was pretty sure she'd made a friend for life.

"It makes me feel so calm, petting her." Avery was surprised to hear herself state the thought out loud, but the combination of the kind stranger's presence and the silky sensation of the dog's warm coat made her feel more at ease than she had since she'd been home.

"She tends to have that effect on people. Lots of dogs do," he said.

Avery looked up to find Isaac beaming with pride, and she noticed again how good-looking he was, in such a different way than the men she'd been attracted to before. His features were less sharp than the square-jawed, light-featured military types she usually preferred. His hair was collar length, wavy and dark, almost black, in the soft glow of lamplight flooding the living room, and his eyes were nearly the same shade of brown. He reminded her of a rakish lord from one of the historical romances she devoured at an incredible pace, one of the few pastimes that allowed her to completely escape the bleak hollows of her own thoughts.

It wouldn't be inaccurate to describe him as *devilishly handsome*, she thought, a smile blossoming over her lips before she caught herself and bit the bottom one.

He caught her smiling and she pretended to study Jane's fur, the heat of a blush rushing to her cheeks. She couldn't remember the last time she'd felt drawn to someone that way, much less *blushed* over a man, for goodness' sake. She'd had a few boyfriends before her first deployment, but it always seemed sort of futile to get into something serious when she'd been on active duty, never knowing when she might have to pack up and leave at last-minute notice. Sure, lots of people made it work, as her mother constantly reminded her, probably with visions of more grandbabies dancing through her head, but Avery had seen enough hurt in that area to last a lifetime.

She swallowed against the dull ache that rose in her heart every time the memory of her best friend crossed her mind, at least a thousand times per day—her punishment for being alive when Sophie was not. Sophie, who'd left behind a husband and child who blamed Avery for Sophie's absence in their lives. It didn't matter whether it had been Avery's fault or not—the center of their world was gone, and Avery had been the last one to see her.

It was Avery who'd promised them she'd watch over their wife and mother, and it was Avery who failed to keep that promise.

She felt Isaac's eyes on her and looked up to meet them.

"You're right about it not being a good idea to walk back in the dark," she admitted. "If it's not too much trouble, I'd like to stick around until the sun comes up, then I'll head back that way."

If Isaac's house was as close to Tommy's as he'd said, it would take her less than ten minutes to jog back at daybreak, and she could slip in the back door and make it into her bed before anyone tried to wake her. Tommy would be making coffee and Macy would be busy with the kids.

He nodded. "Not a problem. If you passed Jane's

character test, then you're welcome to stick around as long as you need to," he said, his tone lighter now. "On one condition."

Avery stopped petting Jane and raised an eyebrow in question.

"Let me cook something for you."

Chapter Three

As he waited for her answer, Isaac glanced at the grandfather clock near the hallway, one of the many things he'd been unable to part with when Nana had willed the old ranch-style home to him a couple of years ago. Its iron hands indicated the hour was near two o'clock in the morning.

They had plenty of time for a bite before daylight when Avery would leave and go back to Dewberry—a thought that, had he more time to entertain, he might have admitted he didn't much care for. He liked the quiet comfort and surrounding memories of the house he'd spent so many happy summers in as a child, and most of the time he was okay with the fact that he lived in the country and didn't entertain a lot of visitors, but there were times when he got lonely. Even though Jane was one hell of a listener, she didn't do much in the way of talking.

It was nice to have a woman in his home. He liked the way Avery's presence added a certain softness to the atmosphere, and he found himself caring whether or not she liked the place.

"I'm not really very hungry," she answered, earning a pointed look from him.

"Come on, now. I'm a very good cook. I'm famous for my barbecue, but I can make a mean sandwich in a pinch. Seriously, call your brother and ask him," Isaac joked, regretting the words when he saw they'd caused her to wince. Tommy had mentioned, of course, that he had a sister who'd recently come home after a few tours in Afghanistan, but since they'd never been introduced or run into each other anywhere in town—which was odd in itself—Isaac hadn't given much thought to the mysterious female Abbott. He and Tommy crossed paths frequently, as the farm always provided food for the events Isaac hosted on behalf of his dog training center, Friends with Fur, but he'd never once seen Avery.

He wouldn't have forgotten her if he had.

The locals talked about her enough; they all had theories about how she might be doing now that she was back, what kind of girl she'd been growing up and—these comments were always in hushed tones accented with the sympathetic clicking of tongues—how she wasn't quite *right* anymore, *bless her heart*. But in Isaac's line of work, he'd learned to withhold judgment until he got to know someone.

And he knew that when broken people kept to themselves, holed up behind walls built to keep out hurt, eventually their family and friends, even the closest ones, stopped asking the hard questions and accepted the new, hollow versions, forgetting that at one time those wounded people were whole.

He got up from his chair and moved toward the couch to scratch Janie's pink tummy, which she'd shamelessly turned over and exposed so that Avery could have the esteemed privilege of rubbing it.

He raised his eyes and watched as Avery pet Jane, admiring the way the dog's gentle serenity seemed to seep into the woman's weary bones.

"Tell you what—I had a long day and I'm hungry, so I'm going to start up a grilled cheese sandwich." He watched Avery for any change in her expression, but her features remained still. "You're welcome to join me if you want to, and I'd be happy to make two."

She raised her eyes then and he was reminded of how blue they were, like shadowy mountaintops at dusk.

"I wasn't always like this, you know," Avery said, her voice so quiet he wasn't sure the words were meant for him to hear.

Even though her gaze was on his, Isaac could tell her thoughts were far off somewhere he couldn't reach. He'd seen the same look on many of the veterans he worked with at the training facility, and he'd learned not to push too hard. Sometimes it was best to stay silent and let the person decide how much he or she wanted to say or not say.

"I used to be strong. Independent." She glanced away. "I can't tell you how humiliating it is to be sitting here in your house, having to trust your word on how I got here."

Isaac's insides ached at her admission and he had the sudden urge to reach out and hold her hand. He wouldn't, but he wanted to.

He'd always had an easier time relating to canines than to his own kind, a product of being homeschooled by a widowed young mom who'd been overwhelmed by the world outside their door, with only his older brother and a series of family pets to keep him company. He would never complain about his childhood. After all, it had been safer and saner than many of his friends' and colleagues', but it had also been lonely.

Ever since he'd moved away briefly for college and then come home to start a business, Isaac had longed for a family of his own. He wanted life to be much different from the way he'd been raised; he wanted kiddos running around shouting happily, dogs barking joyfully and, above all, lots and lots of laughter.

Most people wanted quiet when they came home at the end of a long workday, he thought with a chuckle, but Isaac craved noise.

He wasn't sure what he could say, but he gave it a try anyway. "I know I don't know you, so my saying so doesn't mean much, but you have nothing to be embarrassed by."

He looked up in time to see Avery shaking her head, but he went on, sharing things he rarely got a chance to. "You served your country with honor, and I can bet you dealt with a lot of things no one should ever have to, but that doesn't mean you're different than any other human being. People aren't meant to be around the things I'm sure you were, and come out the same on the other side. War is bound to do some damage to a person's soul. I don't think anyone expects you to come back and pick up where you left off without a few hurdles to jump."

Avery closed her eyes and then opened them slowly, regarding him with an expression he couldn't read.

"Sometimes it feels like that's exactly what they expect."

"Well, they shouldn't," he responded. "And I think that's just a product of not really being able to understand what you went through over there."

Not wanting to say anything that would make Avery uncomfortable, that would make her retreat back into her shell, Isaac gave Jane one final pat and then headed off to the kitchen.

He'd pulled cheese and butter out of the fridge and was opening a wooden bread box when he heard her soft footsteps behind him. He tossed a welcome grin over his shoulder, pleased when he noticed that she wasn't alone. Jane, his big, goofy sweetheart, had followed Avery and was glued to her side. It was one of the characteristics he loved most about dogs. They were quick to make friends.

"How are you so wise about this stuff?" Avery asked, giving him a sad little smile. "Did you serve, as well?"

He shook his head. "No, but in my work, I meet a lot of people who did, and I've learned a few things along the way." He bit back the urge to mention the brother he'd lost; talking about what happened to Stephen would likely be unhelpful at that particular moment.

Her eyes, huge and dark blue in a small, lovely, heart-shaped face, were full of questions and she seemed almost eager, for the first time that evening, to talk with him.

"What kind of work do you do?" she asked, not meeting his eyes as she ran a finger along the glossy edge of the oak table in the adjoining breakfast nook.

"I own a dog-training facility. I opened it a couple of years ago and I have a few assistants now, other trainers. We do all kinds of work—basic obedience, scent, search and rescue—but my most recent project is working with veterans."

"Do you mind if I ask, I mean, how well does that usually work? The vet-and-dog combination?"

Out of the corner of his eye, he watched her sit down at the table and he began cutting squares of cheese off a block of cheddar.

Isaac gave a rough little laugh. "You're not the only one who wants to know that," he said. A lot of people—influential people—wondered the same thing, and soon Isaac hoped to have a way of answering that with his own research, so that he could raise the necessary funding to expand his project. A project that, thanks to great dogs and veterans willing to work hard to overcome their pain, had already changed several lives for the better. He enjoyed all kinds of training, but this particular sort had become his passion over the past couple of years.

"Quite well, actually."

Avery's forehead wrinkled in curiosity, which he took as an invitation to keep talking. Normally, he was a pretty quiet guy, even a little on the shy side, one might say, but when it came to his career, he could go on all day.

"Service animals make some of the best companions to soldiers who've returned from war carrying more than physical baggage. With the right training, they can be a huge asset to people dealing with past trauma or symptoms of PTSD, and they can be even better than medication at calming soldiers in the midst of panic attacks, or…even flashbacks."

He wasn't going to put a label on what had happened with Avery that night. He wasn't a doctor and he didn't have all the details, but his gut told him that's what had occurred to her prior to him stumbling upon her in that ditch.

"Sorry if I sound like a public service announcement. I just care a lot about this stuff. It's affected a lot of people I care about."

Her shoulders let go of some of their tension as he spoke, and there was even a hint of hope in her eyes as he explained the process of rescuing dogs from the local shelter and giving them homes, purpose and new, full lives.

"So basically you're saving two people at once," she said, her eyes brighter than they had been since he'd met her. "Or, well, one person and one dog—you know what I meant," she said, her cheeks turning a pretty, soft pink.

He bent to pull a skillet from a low cabinet, partly so he could warm up a pat of butter and start the sandwich, and partly so she wouldn't see the way her sweet expression had affected him.

He didn't mind helping her out—any decent guy

would have done the same—and he was glad to let her stay awhile until the sun came up. He was even happy to make her a much-needed meal. He told himself it was harmless to feel attracted to a too-thin but still gorgeous woman he'd happened upon by some stroke of fate, but what he could not allow was for that attraction to go any further.

From the looks of things, Avery Abbott needed a lot of help, some of which he might even be able to offer, but it was highly unlikely she was looking for a relationship. Not with what she was obviously going through right now.

And Isaac, truth be told, very much wanted one.

He lit the stove and waited for it to heat, finally placing the butter in to melt.

"I haven't saved anyone," he said. "They save each other."

While the butter changed from solid to a sizzling little pool, he put cheese between bread slices and arranged two plates to hold the finished food. Once he'd set the first sandwich in the pan, he chanced another look at her, surprised to see unshed tears shimmering in Avery's eyes. She rubbed at her lids and he looked away, kicking himself for saying something that might have added any more pain to her already awful night. He wanted to apologize, but wasn't sure what to say; words had never been his strong suit. He much preferred movement and action, but those weren't always what was required.

Five minutes later, he plated the sandwiches and brought them, along with two glasses of water, over to the table to join Avery, who smiled up at him as he sat, all traces of moisture gone from those sapphire eyes.

"Thank you for this," she said softly, "and for everything. I owe you one."

"You don't owe me anything," he said. "What was I supposed to do, leave you out there alone on the side of the road? What kind of man would that make me?" He winked and picked up his sandwich.

That coaxed a little grin out of her, which gave him more satisfaction than it should have.

"I have to say, Mr. Meyer, you do seem like a stand-up guy. Do you make a habit of rescuing lost women in the middle of the night?" she asked, and he had the distinct feeling she was flirting with him a little.

Something fluttered in his belly, and he didn't think it was hunger.

"I haven't before," he answered, "but after tonight, who knows? Maybe I will."

Avery laughed so hard at that cheesiness that the sip of water she'd just taken almost came out of her nose. Within minutes, they were both laughing like idiots, at what he really couldn't say.

But it felt good.

After the weirdest night of his life, and after the too-strong sense of relief he now felt seeing that this woman, this soldier, could still laugh despite the things life had thrown her way, it felt good to join her in a moment of ridiculousness. It was almost as if something in his heart had come unknotted.

Even though he knew it was completely irrational, he realized suddenly, with as much certainty and force as one might realize it's raining as drops hit the ground, that he would do absolutely everything he could to help her get better.

Chapter Four

Avery's heart hammered out a quick rhythm as she opened the back door slowly and with measured care—then winced as it squeaked loudly in protest, as if its intention was to inform the entire house of her... adventures.

She resented feeling like a teenager, sneaking into her brother's home. Just another reminder that her life as of late was anything but normal. And, oh, how she craved normal.

"Morning, sweetheart."

Despite its softness, Macy's greeting caused Avery to gasp and turn around so fast that whiplash wouldn't have been an implausible outcome.

"Holy goodness, Mace. You scared the living daylights out of me," Avery said, shoving a hand against her heart. As she leaned back and let her spine rest against the closed door, fighting to catch her breath, she studied her sister-in-law. Macy was, as always, as pretty at the crack of dawn—with her golden hair all messy and the imprint of a pillow seam etched into her cheek—as she had been on her and Tommy's wedding day. Avery indulged in the memory—a time when everything was simpler, purer—before she'd brought home a personal hell that had begun to seep into all their lives.

"Speaking of daylights," Macy said quietly, tugging her frayed, pink terry-cloth robe tighter around her waist, "the sun hasn't even risen and here you are looking like you've had quite a night."

Avery's lips formed a thin line, but she held Macy's gaze, despite the temptation to look away from what she saw in the sweet, open face.

"What do you want me to say?"

Macy closed her eyes and then opened them again, sympathy etched into her features. "I just want you to be okay, honey, that's all. We all do." She looked as though she might want to touch or hold Avery, but knew better from experience.

Even though the conversation wasn't anything new, something tugged at Avery's heartstrings and for a second she longed to just collapse and let it all out—to tell someone how desperately scared she was, how the nightmares kept getting worse, and how she couldn't always tell the difference between those and the flashbacks. How sometimes she wasn't sure whether she was awake or asleep.

But something else, something strange and new, told

her this wasn't the time or place…but that maybe she was getting close to being able to do just that…and that maybe Isaac was that place. As Macy waited for an answer to the questions she hadn't voiced out loud but were always there, Avery thought back to the man she'd met that morning.

Even under the strange circumstances that brought them together last night, he had been so calm, so sturdy and safe, like a lighthouse in a raging storm. He'd taken care of her without hesitation, and for some reason she knew he would have done the same for any wayward creature.

He was the embodiment of that most rare and beautiful thing, something Avery had seen precious little of over the past few years: basic human kindness.

"Well, now, there's something you don't see every day," Macy said, a giggle bubbling up around her words. "You want to tell me what has you smiling like that, or is it a secret?"

Avery, disbelieving, reached up and touched a finger to her lips, realizing only upon feeling their upward curve to what her sister-in-law referred. Before she could form a response, Macy's eyes lit up and her mouth opened wide.

"Oh, my gosh, Avery," she blurted. "Were you—" she crossed her arms over her chest and leaned forward "—were you…with a guy?"

"No!" Avery spat, but she wasn't fooling anyone. She winced. "Well, technically, yes, but it's not what it seems." She held her palms out, hoping for emphasis.

Macy eyed her with blatant skepticism. "Yeah," she

said, grinning, "usually when people say that, it's exactly what it seems."

A little unexpected laugh escaped from Avery's throat. She peered at her sister, her friend, with narrow eyes. "You've been watching too many romantic comedies," she said, hoping to divert attention away from herself, blushing a little at the mere thought that Macy's suggestion put into her head.

She had a feeling it wouldn't go away as easily or as quickly as it had arrived. Isaac's dark, unruly hair twisted around her fingers, those deep brown eyes gazing at her with...with what, exactly? Lust? Over *her*?

Not likely, at least not in her current state of skin and bones. She'd need to put on a good ten pounds before anything like that happened, or someone might get hurt. Before she could stop them, more thoughts tumbled in, unbidden. Suddenly, she remembered being carried in those arms—strong arms, brandished a deep gold by the Texas sun—and, for once, the thought of being held didn't seem quite so scary. It was nice to feel attraction to a man, a welcome distraction from her usual preoccupations.

"Something tells me I'm not too far off," Macy said, interrupting Avery's ridiculous reverie.

It would be great if her dreams were more like that than the terrifying things they actually were. She met her sister-in-law's curious gaze. "No," she answered truthfully. "I did run into your neighbor Isaac Meyer, but it's not like what you're thinking."

Macy's shoulders sagged and Avery's heart bruised.

How desperately she longed to bring smiles to her loved ones' faces—not pain or disappointment.

Macy reached out a hand, tentatively, and after a second's hesitation, Avery grabbed it, anxiety and a desire for comfort raging a familiar battle at the sensation of human contact. Macy's expression registered the wound, but there wasn't much to say on the subject that hadn't already been rehashed a hundred times.

Her family knew she'd suffered plenty of emotional trauma during her last tour; she spared them the details of what happened in that place. She knew that these people who loved her were not the enemy. She knew they meant her no harm, but her body, and parts of her mind, still struggled with the difference between a friendly touch and a hostile one.

"I'd be lying if I said it wouldn't be nice to see you spending some time with a sweet fella," Macy answered. "Isaac Meyer definitely fits the bill, and that boy has been single for way too long." She gently squeezed Avery's hand before tugging her in the direction of the kitchen. "Come on. Let's get some caffeine in you and you can tell me what exactly did happen."

She winked and Avery rolled her eyes, but allowed herself to be led toward the energizing scent of fresh coffee.

Maybe it wouldn't hurt for her to talk to Macy about the strange past few hours. Maybe it would be nice to share breakfast and silly, carefree chatter about a man, like the old days.

Or at least she could pretend to, for her family's sake.

* * *

"All set?" Macy asked later that morning as Avery stepped into the lobby following her weekly appointment with Dr. Santiago, her therapist.

Avery nodded and Macy smiled warmly as she put down a magazine she'd been reading, grabbed her purse and stood to leave. They walked quietly to the elevator, Avery reviewing her session with Dr. Santiago. Though she saw the doctor regularly, most of her previous appointments ran together, characterized only by the strong feeling that nothing ever really changed; some days were better than others, but overall, she felt she'd made no true progress over the past several months, a thought that only served to decrease her confidence that she would someday get past it all.

But today—something felt different. Something felt...better. She couldn't quite put her finger on it. Was it that she had tried harder to talk about her struggles? Had she simply opened up more? Yes, and no. She shook her head as she reached out to punch the down button on the panel between two elevators. Perhaps she'd made a little more effort than usual to speak frankly with the doctor, but it wasn't just that. She always did her best during her sessions, always pushed as far as she could go, working to excavate that deep abyss of painful war memories. No. This time, it was something else. Something to do with her night with Isaac.

"So, I was thinking," Macy said, her words tentative, almost as though she knew before she spoke them that whatever idea she had would be shot down. Avery winced, fully aware that she had a large part in making her sister-in-law feel that way around her.

Avery looked over to see Macy fiddling with her purse strap, her forehead creased. "What is it?"

"Well, you know that new nail salon they just opened up the street from here?"

"Uh-huh," Avery answered, her thoughts still partly focused on her session with Dr. Santiago. She heard Macy swallow.

"I was thinking we could stop on the way to the grocery and maybe get pedicures or something." She looked over at Avery, cautious hope in her eyes. "My treat."

A sharp *ding* sound rang out and the elevator doors slid open. Once they'd stepped inside and chosen the ground floor as their destination, Avery glanced over at Macy, who was biting her lower lip now, her features giving away her trepidation.

Avery's heart sank. How many times had she said no to such a simple request, to things that Macy offered as a way to reach out to her, in constant effort to help her through her tough times? How many times had she denied those offers, yet they kept coming? She smiled softly at Macy, realizing for the first time how lucky she was to have this persistent, positive woman in her life. How many others had she hurt and pushed away because she was too afraid they wouldn't be able to handle the new, dark parts of her soul?

"I'd like that," she said, and Macy's face lit up. Macy squeezed her palms and raised her forearms, then lowered them quickly so as not to appear too excited.

"It's okay," Avery said, giggling. "You can be happy about it."

"Yay!" Macy cried out as she did a little bounce, causing them both to laugh.

The elevator stopped and both women stepped out into the parking garage.

"Look, Macy, I know it must be hard for you to keep…trying…with me, and—" Avery swallowed over the lump developing in her throat, startled by the sudden onslaught of emotion "—I want you to know I notice how hard you've been trying to make me feel better." She closed her eyes, working to organize her thoughts around the most important thing she needed to get across. "I mean to say that I'm thankful for you. For all that you and Tommy do for me, really. But especially you."

Macy stopped and turned toward Avery, her eyes filling as she reached out and wrapped her sister-in-law in a hug, squeezing hard.

When she let go, they walked to the car in silence, both smiling. It felt good to say yes to something, even something as small as a pedicure with a special family member—and friend—who'd remained close, no matter how hard Avery unintentionally pushed her away. She thought of that night with Isaac, how she'd allowed him to feed and care for her, despite feeling afraid of what conclusions he might draw about the state of her mental health. It was almost as though that choice—the choice to let someone new in, despite the difficulty it took to do so—was an opening for other opportunities that she'd been missing out on for so long.

Besides, she thought, grinning to herself, she could use some color on her toes. She decided then that she would pick something bright, something that would make her feel uplifted when she looked down at her feet. Something that maybe Isaac might notice and like.

As Macy pulled her car out into the sunshine, a small spark of life lit up somewhere deep inside the darkest place in Avery's heart.

Chapter Five

What had seemed like a good idea earlier that morning was really just a sack of zucchini in the light of day.

Isaac could have kicked his own ass for not coming up with a better ruse for stopping by to check on Avery Abbott after the night they'd spent in each other's company. A week had passed since that strange night—the slowest week of his life. He'd only been able to go through the motions during that time, each task permeated with thoughts of a woman unlike any other he'd ever met.

But still…zucchini? Anyone would be able to see through his excuse. The vegetable was insanely easy to grow, even in a dry-as-a-bone Texas summer like the one they were having—they were so good at growing that anyone within a hundred miles of Peach Leaf who wanted the vegetables already had enough to feed an army. People could only stand so many salads and breads and desserts with the stuff snuck in. But, for some knuckleheaded reason, Isaac had decided that bringing a bag of the green things would pass as a decent excuse to visit his neighbor's farm.

Yes, that's correct, he thought. *I'm bringing a crap ton of zucchini...to a farm*. He shook his head. Hell, it might have *come* from that very farm, he noted with a sinking sensation in his belly.

With so many well-meaning locals—overwhelmingly widows and grannies...and widowed grannies—dropping off food at his place on a regular basis, he lost track of its origins. He didn't hold it against all the sweet gals, but once in a while, it was enough to make him consider moving to Austin, where a thirtysomething bachelor wasn't likely to turn so many heads.

He pulled his four-wheeler into Tommy and Macy's drive, careful to watch out for free-range chickens and goats. He got out and Jane jumped down from her perch on the seat in front of him, hightailing it up the porch steps. As the front door swung open, the scent of something sweet cooking wafted out into the already warm air.

"Hey, Janie girl," Tommy said, scratching the dog between her ears before she invited herself into the house. "Hey, bud," he said, turning to Isaac and heading down the steps, cup of coffee in hand.

"Mornin', Tom," Isaac said, returning the greeting as he reached into the seat compartment to pull out the embarrassing sack of vegetables.

Tommy's eyebrows rose up so far they almost met

the brim of his straw Stetson. When Isaac just stood there, holding the offending sack away from him like a baby with a dirty diaper, realization crossed Tommy's features and he started to slowly back away, holding up a hand. "Aw, no way, man. Macy's got so many of those damn things. If she strung all the little bastards together, they'd reach the moon and back."

Isaac cursed and swung the bag over his shoulder, feeling more and more like a complete idiot.

"What in the world were you thinking bringing those things here?" Tommy continued, keeping his distance. "You lost your ever-lovin' mind, my friend?" He took a long sip of his coffee, clearly waiting for a response.

The two men had been good friends ever since Isaac inherited his grandma's property and moved in to the old ranch house. They were living proof that opposites really do attract. Isaac, who wasn't usually keen on too much chatter, had taken an instant liking to his neighbor, despite the fact that the man never shut his mouth and could carry on a conversation with just about anybody or anything. His easygoing habit of yakking made Isaac comfortable, mostly because he didn't have to say much for them to get along just fine, and, well, Tommy was just so damn nice. Also, it was obvious that the man doted on his family, as if Macy had hung the moon, and their two little ones, all the stars in the sky.

It was exactly the kind of family Isaac had always pictured having himself one day. If only he could find the right girl. Someone who wouldn't mind his quiet nature and his shyness around new people. Someone, maybe, kind of like Avery Abbott—his true reason for dropping by.

"Oh, just forget about those things and come on in. Macy's got breakfast on. But, if you think it's just flour, milk and sugar in those waffles, guess again. It's like I said before, that girl has stuffed those green devils into everything we've eaten in the past month because she hates to waste them, and, I'm telling you, at least fifty more popped up in her garden overnight."

Isaac smiled at his friend's happy chatter.

"Don't be surprised if next time you stop by, I've turned into one of 'em." Tommy stopped suddenly at the top of the steps. "What'd you say you dropped by for, again?" He lifted up his white hat and scratched his forehead. "Not that you need a reason. Just want to make sure you don't leave here empty-handed if you were needing something—"

"Tom?" Isaac said quietly, seeking a brief break in his friend's out-loud thinking.

"—Macy would never let me hear the end of it if—"

"Tom!"

He finally turned around, a sleepy smile on his face. Isaac had never known his friend to wear any other expression.

"What's on your mind, bud?"

Now that he had Tom's attention, Isaac hesitated, unsure what can of worms he might risk opening if he answered the question truthfully.

He knew Tom was protective of Avery beyond what would be expected of a brother, and he could understand why. From what he'd seen the other night, what folks said about her time in service, and from the way she seemed to socialize far less than other locals, he could guess that she'd come back from war bearing a few scars—the kind you couldn't see with a good pair of eyes.

The jumpiness he'd witnessed in her that night and her disorientation in an area she was familiar with were textbook post-trauma symptoms. He recognized them from the vets he trained service dogs for, and from— the memory still ached in a part of Isaac's heart that he knew would never heal—from his brother. Which was why he'd avoided visiting the farm and his friends the past few months since he'd heard that Avery moved in. Working with PTSD victims in his job was one thing— watching his friend's sister struggle through it was entirely another.

She needed help. More help than whatever Veteran Affairs currently provided, more help than her family would know how to give her, regardless of how much they loved and supported her.

Isaac knew, better than most, that love wasn't always enough.

Love couldn't always save someone.

So, as much as it might cost him in the long run, Isaac decided it was best to be open with Tom, for Avery's sake. He'd just have to make sure Macy didn't read too much into his visit, or she'd be on his case, and he'd find himself being set up again, only to turn up disappointed if it didn't work out.

The other night, despite her condition, he could feel the electric hint of possibility between them, and he couldn't deny that she was the prettiest woman he'd ever laid eyes on—but for now, all he wanted to do was help.

He set his shoulders back and held up a hand to shade his brow against the first rays of the rising sun. The day was already plenty warm, and he could tell it would be a hot one.

"Actually, yeah. There is something on my mind. Two things, actually. I'm so sorry I haven't stopped by to see you guys lately, and, well, I'm not here to see you now, to be honest."

Isaac ignored the goofy grin on Tommy's face, not really caring that he wasn't making any sense.

"I'm here to check on Avery."

Avery accepted the mug Macy handed her and took a long sip of the rich, strong coffee it contained, closing her eyes as the taste of good beans, a little sugar and a splash of fresh cream washed over her taste buds.

Macy was grinning from across the table when she opened her eyes.

"Good?"

"The best. I've always loved your coffee. Not like the coffee-flavored water Tommy always made before you came along," Avery said, laughing.

Macy beamed with pride. "Well, I'm glad you like it, and it's here every morning, but it's not enough to put meat on your bones, girl. You can't keep going on caffeine and the occasional bowl of cereal. You need to eat. You've barely had a real meal since you moved in here."

Avery took another sip and nodded in agreement. "I know I do."

"So, tell me what it is. Is there something I can make that you'd wolf down? When I first met Tommy, you were a nachos-and-beer kind of girl. Maybe we just need to get you to a Tex-Mex place, stat." Macy's voice was light, but Avery didn't miss the hint of seriousness in the woman's words.

"It's hard to explain, Mace. It's almost like…like everything tastes stale or cardboard-y. I couldn't tell you why. Ever since… I just can't seem to eat like I used to. But I'll try harder. Really, I will. And last week, I did eat a pretty mean sandwich at Isaac's—"

At the sound of the front door swinging open, both women exchanged glances and then turned their heads to the kitchen entryway.

"Honey, is that you?" Macy called out.

"Me and company," Tommy bellowed from the hallway.

A racket started at the front door and thundered down the hall, and suddenly Isaac's dog, Jane, was rushing through the kitchen entrance, headed straight toward the table. Macy's eyes widened in surprise but Avery's heart swelled at the sight of the dog.

"Janie!" Avery said as the giant mutt bounded over to her chair. She stopped short and sat in front of Avery, her behind wiggling with the effort of not jumping into Avery's lap. She reached up a paw and Avery touched it, laughing. "High-five!"

"Goodness," Macy said. "Someone's in love."

"Who's in love?" Tommy asked, entering the kitchen and heading over to kiss the top of his wife's head, then on to the coffeepot. "Mornin', sweetie. Mornin', Ave," he said as Isaac sidled up behind him to prop a shoulder against the doorway, arms crossed over his broad chest.

Avery's breath caught at the sight of him. Good Lord, he was even better looking in the morning light: shoulder-length hair still unruly but obviously moist and gleaming from a shower, dark eyes glittering as they met hers. He was dressed in faded jeans and a cobalt-blue T-shirt that brought out the olive tones in his sun-kissed skin.

"Avery," he said, his voice velvety-soft. He nodded at her, his lips offering just a hint of a grin, and, if she hadn't been sitting in a chair, she was fairly certain she'd have melted into a puddle right there on the kitchen floor.

Thankfully, he turned from her to say good morning to his hostess, who jumped up from the table to give him a big hug. "Isaac," Macy said, squeezing his midsection before turning to get him a cup of coffee. "It's so good to see you. You've been such a stranger lately." She held him at arm's length so she could get a good look at him. "I've told Tom to head on over and check on you and Jane, but he insisted you've been fine, just busy.

"And he's right," Isaac reassured her. "But I do appreciate you thinking of me."

Macy let go of him and picked up the carafe to pour him a mug, and, without asking how he took it, left it black and set it at the place next to Avery on the round, antique oak table. She winked and Avery felt her cheeks warm.

They'd been talking about him just before.

He walked in. As he drew near and pulled out the

chair only inches away from hers, Avery had to remind herself that he wasn't aware of that fact.

It was true that her family had spent a lot of energy worrying about her lately. She'd been back home for almost six months and dutifully kept her appointments with her therapist at the VA clinic in downtown Peach Leaf, but her symptoms weren't going away; in fact, they hadn't even gotten better. Sometimes, she thought, they seemed to be getting worse.

And with each flashback, each nightmare, each— her favorite—panic attack, Avery lost more and more of her self-esteem.

Where was the strong woman who'd enlisted after nursing school, hoping to see the world and serve her country as a medical professional? Where was the girl who'd always been drawn to the needs of others, to healing broken bodies?

She couldn't help anyone in her current state—least of all, herself—and it killed her a little more each day.

Avery hadn't realized it, as lost as she'd been in her own thoughts, but when she looked up, she met Jane's brown eyes, and noticed that her hand was buried in the dog's fur, stroking it. The repetitive movement and the feel of the satiny coat soothed her. If she focused on that motion instead of the turbulence inside her mind, things began to settle down.

She turned to Isaac and he met her eyes. There was a gentle smile in them that made her think maybe it wouldn't be so hard to try, just a little.

"I've always liked dogs so much," she said, still petting Jane, who promptly rolled over to expose her pink belly.

Avery and Isaac both laughed.

"She's a big, spoiled-rotten ham," he said. "A very good girl, don't get me wrong. But spoiled nonetheless."

"No way," Avery said, defending her new best friend from Isaac's good-humored chiding. "She's a sweetheart."

"Ha! She's got you wrapped around her paw there, I see," Isaac answered, shaking his head.

Macy informed him he'd be staying on for breakfast and it didn't take too long for him to give up his protest that he had work to do and didn't want to be in their hair all morning. Finally, he agreed to stay for waffles. Avery's niece and nephew joined the adults, rubbing their eyes from sleep. She snuck kisses on their matching strawberry-smelling, soft, flyaway blond hair before they saw Jane and ran over excitedly to pet the dog, completely ignoring everyone else in the room until Macy gently scolded them to say hello to Mr. Isaac. They did, before promptly returning their attention to Jane.

Avery chuckled. The dog *was* indeed spoiled, but she deserved it.

Tommy headed off to wash up from the morning's milking, which he always did alongside his six hired hands, and Macy busied herself with the waffle batter.

"You're a natural with Jane," Isaac said as she set places with plates and utensils, then sat back down at the table, having been shooed away from her offers to help Macy prepare breakfast. "Mind if I ask why you don't have one of your own?"

Avery fingered the yellow stars that decorated her favorite black coffee mug. "Well, I haven't really given it much thought," she answered, noticing that Isaac's eyes traveled over her face with intensity that made her both extremely flattered and disconcerted. As one of just a couple of females among the majority of males that had made up her team, she wasn't used to such attention. She was used to being just one of the guys. Part of her thoroughly enjoyed the way those brown eyes studied her features with obvious interest; another part warned her to turn and run. She wasn't relationship material—now or possibly ever. Too much baggage. Too much damage.

"Before I went into the army, I was a nurse, and my shifts didn't allow time for me to be a good pet owner." Nervous, she tucked a strand of hair behind her ear, wondering, for the first time in a long time, how it looked and when was the last time she'd brushed it or had a proper trim. It occurred to her that it wouldn't hurt to ask her stylist friend Jessica if she could squeeze in an appointment during the upcoming week.

A little change might make her feel better.

Isaac nodded, so she continued. "Then, when I joined, well…that's no mystery." She offered a soft smile. "I wouldn't have wanted to leave a pet behind for my family to care for in my absence, and I'm enough of a burden on them as it is for me to bring someone else into their home."

Wow. Her mother would turn over in her grave if

she'd heard Avery sharing something so private with a relative stranger. The thing was, though, he didn't feel much like a stranger.

She turned quickly away and stared into her coffee mug. But before her eyes had left his, she'd seen the flash of sadness on Isaac's features and chided herself to be more careful; she didn't want him feeling sorry for her. Him or anyone else.

"Sounds to me like you'd make a wonderful pet owner," he said, surprising her. "You've obviously thought through these things, which is more than I can say for a lot of people."

"What do you mean?" she asked, unable to keep her eyes from him. Something about the man drew her in, and the more time she spent around him, the more she realized his company was like a balm to her frayed nerves. He was like a dip in cool spring water on a hot summer day, and she'd have to be very, very cautious to avoid getting pulled under.

"Just that a lot of people get pets, especially dogs, thinking that the animals will just be happy to have a home and food, but they need so much more than that. They need love and attention and medical care and training. They're incredibly wonderful, but a big responsibility. Most people don't think about all of those things, but it's obvious that you have, and I just think you'd be a wonderful dog mom if you ever decided that you wanted to be."

He gave her another one of those sweet but sexy grins—the kind that made her forget she was in a room full of other people, full of her family and full of the morning chaos of another busy day. Though she was apparently the only Abbott born with a black thumb, Avery did her best to help out around the farm—watching the kids so Macy could bake or have some time to herself, riding one of the horses out to check fences and crops with one or two of the hands, or helping Tommy with the milking.

Six months ago, when she'd come to live with her brother and his family, she'd thought that kind of work would save her from the persistent, dark memories she'd brought home from war. But now, after living through several months of hard, manual labor–filled days, she knew it wasn't enough. It was just another kind of running. She could cover a thousand miles, and those same memories would always be one step ahead of her, ready to knock her back down into the pit.

But something about Isaac's compliment, about the idea of a dog, sparked her interest. Something about the thought of having a living thing to take care of—one that was all her own—offered an inkling of hope. But with hope came the risk of opening up, of putting her heart out there, and she wasn't quite sure she could do it just yet. Still, maybe if she took the tiniest of steps in that direction...

She cleared her throat and looked back to Isaac, who was draining the last of his coffee. "Tommy tells me you've helped a lot of vets with your training," she said, her voice sounding uncertain even to her own ears. "I'd love to hear more about it."

"Well, I'm certified in general canine training, and I do all kinds of basic and advanced behavioral training, plus some search and rescue and drug-finding stuff for the local sheriff's department, and I do work with vets sometimes, mostly pairing them with companion animals that we all feel are a good fit. Then I tailor the training to whatever a client's particular needs are. I've taken several courses in training therapy dogs, but I'm always learning more, especially from working directly with veterans."

He stopped there and she could tell he was trying not to bore or overwhelm her, which shouldn't surprise her after the other night. Most people would have labeled her crazy and gone on about their business. Isaac was different. He was testing the waters and giving her room to go at her own pace, to seek information rather than being force-fed facts. It was a relief after all of the VA appointments and therapy sessions.

"What happens then?"

Isaac's brow furrowed. "Well, as you've seen with Jane, dogs can be very calming. They can relax us when we're getting to that breaking point where nothing's helping and we just need a lifeline—someone to pull us back from the edge. All dogs, all breeds, have the potential to be amazing with humans, given a chance. But they're just like people in that they don't all get along. Not every dog likes every other dog, and not every dog is right for every person. It's a matter of finding the right dog for the right vet. When that happens, it's incredible what they can do for each other."

Okay, now she was really interested.

As a waffle-filled plate appeared in front of her, Avery looked up to find Macy smiling. She rolled her eyes but the truth was, she was glad to have someone to talk to who didn't seem to judge her. Someone who had seen one of her worst episodes and hadn't overreacted or, well, freaked out the way most people did. She was lucky Isaac was the one who'd found her wandering around in the darkness. It could have been anyone—but it was him. He'd taken care of her as though she belonged to him, as though she was his to keep safe and protect. And, because of his work, which she'd grilled Macy about the week before—something she'd made her sister-in-law swear to secrecy—he had the knowledge and experience to maybe help her, or to at least be her friend.

After what they'd been through in just a short amount of time, Avery knew he wouldn't scare easy the way most people did. She didn't blame them, really. It usually was just a matter of not knowing what to say, not knowing how to talk to her about her experiences in a combat zone most had only seen on edited television. Still, it hurt that her old friends seemed almost…afraid of her, as though she might break at any moment. And, to be fair, she could.

But Isaac wasn't like that. He was gentle and careful with her, but at the same time, he didn't treat her with kid gloves. He'd gotten her to talk more about her problems last week than her therapist had in months of trying different approaches. Plus, the idea that he could somehow even help her to get better—could maybe even work with a dog to help her—brought her more optimism than she'd felt since coming home, and she was smart enough not to resist a good thing when she saw it.

Also, it didn't hurt the situation that he was the most ruggedly beautiful man she'd ever seen.

"I want to know more," she said, pushing her shoulders back and meeting his eyes, a dose of bravery coursing through her veins. "How do I do that?"

Isaac's eyes flashed with interest and pride as he swallowed the bite of waffles he'd taken and set down his fork. Avery noticed that he'd finished over half of the food on his plate while she hadn't eaten a single morsel. "First, you eat."

"Oh," she said, looking down at her food. It did look good, but she knew that when she put a forkful into her mouth, it would taste like nothing. "I'm not really hungry."

He pulled a face that told her he wasn't buying the excuse. "All right, Abbott. Let's make a deal."

The twinkle in his eyes sent an arrow through that surge of bravery she'd felt only a moment before, but she wouldn't let him see. Over three tours, she'd had plenty of practice pretending to possess courage when in fact she did not. "Fine."

"Good," Isaac said, folding his hands in his lap. "Eat at least half of those waffles, and instead of telling you more about my training, I'll do you one better."

"How's that?" she asked, eyeing her food, deciding if she was really up for the challenge.

"You can come in to the office with me tomorrow."

"You've got work tomorrow?" she asked, and he nodded. "It's Saturday. I thought only us farm folks and emergency professionals had to report for duty so early on the weekend."

Isaac smiled and his eyes crinkled at the corners, lending sweetness to his sharp features.

"Yes, well, running a small business means there's always work to be done, and even when I do take a day off, it's hard not to think about all the things I could be doing."

"Sounds like a lot to handle," said Avery.

He nodded but his eyes held only satisfied joy, and she found she wanted to learn more about something that brought such contentment to his life.

"It is that, but I absolutely love the work. I opened the training center a couple of years back when my grandmother left me her house and land here. And, after having worked a corporate desk job since college, I'll never go back. Being my own boss and setting my own schedule is the best thing in the world."

"Even when you have to work weekends?" Avery asked, grinning.

"Even then," he said, returning her grin.

Isaac's eyes lit up when he talked about his work, and his enthusiasm got her excited about the opportunity to see where he spent his days. But, behind all of that, a little bit of sadness stung inside her chest. She missed her own work. She missed her patients at the hospital, her daily rounds and having the chance to give back to her community by caring for people. For Avery, being a nurse was more than just a job—it was a calling, something that filled her soul. And, even more simply, she felt lost without the daily routine of getting up and driving into town.

She'd tried to build a new life for herself on the farm

after the incident she'd had at work. It still made her face burn to remember her boss finding her huddled up in the corner of a patient's room, having mistaken the sound of a dropped food tray for an explosion. The resulting mandatory vacation leave her boss had ordered was justified, but it wasn't easy adjusting to time away from work. Despite pushing herself for long hours in the Texas sun to help her brother, she felt useless there. It would never be enough to replace nursing.

"Did I say something wrong?" Isaac asked, worry lines etching the dark skin of his forehead.

"No, no," she answered, surprising them both when she reached out and gently lay a hand across one of his. Even more startling was the absence of need to pull it away.

Isaac looked at their hands, then back at Avery, before winding his fingers through hers. The motion pulled all of the air from her lungs for just a second, but she didn't flinch.

Be brave, she told herself. *It's just a friendly gesture. It's just ordinary human contact.*

And, much to her pleased relief, it worked. As she allowed him to hold her hand, ignoring everything else in the room, her fear trickled away drop by drop. It was, after all, just a hand—but it belonged to Isaac, which made it okay somehow. Safe, steady Isaac.

She thought suddenly of the towering stack of historical romance paperbacks on her night table, of all the ways the authors described the heroes therein. In those books that she loved so much, the rakes and Vikings were always full of adventure and the promise of pulse-pounding, high-stakes danger, and though Avery could lose herself in those stories for hours, she'd always had difficulty relating to heroines who would want all of those things, when she herself craved just the opposite.

To Avery, the most romantic thing in the world was also the simplest: a partner who provided a safe home, gentle hands, stability and unconditional love.

She'd had enough adventure to last a lifetime, and all she really wanted now was a soft place to land.

She hadn't spent much time before, considering what that might look like in her own life, but seeing Isaac's hand wrapped around her own and the warm affection swimming in his dark eyes, she was starting to get a pretty good idea.

Avery cleared her throat and shook her head. "No, you didn't say anything wrong." She gave his hand a little squeeze. "I was just thinking about my own job, hearing you talk about how much you enjoy yours."

He was silent for a moment, just looking at her, no judgment discernible in his expression. When he spoke, his voice was kind but determined. "Listen, Abbott," he said, "whatever happened to you over there, whatever made you stop doing something you love, you can't let that make you quit for good. If you want to go back to nursing, or even train for a different career, you absolutely can. And I think I can help."

No hesitation, no "Let's take things slow," no "Maybe someday in the future"—none of the platitudes she was so used to hearing—just pure confidence in her ability to help herself get better.

It must have been exactly what she needed to hear,

because in just a short time with Isaac Meyer, she felt better than she had in months. And to think he'd been there all along, just a short walk up the road.

She was tired of taking baby steps and getting nowhere, tired of carefully stepping on stones across a deep abyss only to fall over and over again, then to face the challenge of climbing back out over slippery walls. Her therapists at the VA were wonderful, and she knew she needed their help to find balance again. But it wasn't enough to commit to doing the mental work; she needed some actionable steps to take in order to feel more than passive in her own journey.

She'd read about service dogs for vets with PTSD, and most of the research was positive. Besides, she had nothing to lose. Everything she'd known before—the life she'd left with when she joined the military—was gone, and she knew it would probably never return. So, if Isaac wanted to help her with this new one, and if the way to do so was by working with a dog, it was worth one hell of a try. She wanted to be whole again, whatever that meant, and she was willing to try something innovative to get there, even if being whole now wouldn't look the same as it had before she'd left.

In fact, she was beginning to hope it didn't, because before, Isaac hadn't been a part of her world, and she'd decided this morning that she very much liked him in it.

Chapter Six

Friends with Fur had started out as just a business for Isaac—a way to earn a living and to get out from behind the desk that he'd sworn at the time would eventually kill him—but in the years since its opening, it had become so much more.

Even looking back on those *before* days from a safe distance made him cringe, and caused a trapped feeling to rise up like a scream from his chest to his throat. He'd been thirty when Nana passed and surprised the hell out of Isaac by leaving him her farm and savings. Inheriting Nana's property shouldn't have come as a shock because his mom hadn't survived her last heart failure, and of course his brother, Stephen, was gone long before that, but it had nonetheless. Suddenly, he'd been given a chance at a new life, and he didn't take that lightly.

After years of working his way up from mail clerk to a corner office at an investment firm in Austin—a relatively reliable job with a steady, respectable paycheck—Isaac had begun to feel the claws of suffocation wrapping around him, longing for days that didn't all look exactly the same as the ones that came before and after. He'd gone to college mostly to please his mother and to get a taste of city life, but everything that followed seemed to rush in as smoothly as though he'd been on autopilot, just following a predetermined set of steps. Internships, job offers and a ladder to climb.

He'd gotten very near the top, but it wasn't enough. When he'd confided in his friends about his increasing longing to do something else, most had responded in the same way his mom had: they'd told him he was lucky to have a high-paying job, and he could do what he pleased as soon as he retired. He knew there was an element of truth in their statements, but there was also fear. Something inside him burned for change, and he didn't want to wait thirty more years to feel that his days had real purpose. Surely, he'd begun to dream, there had to be some way to earn a living doing something he loved. And just when he'd worked up the courage to take a leave of absence to try and figure out what to do about his future, Nana had gotten sick.

He'd come back to Peach Leaf to take care of her and to make certain she lived her final days in peaceful comfort. When she breathed her last, she gave him a new beginning. The farmhouse where he'd spent his summers was old, but in decent shape, and with Nana's life savings, he'd fixed it up and studied to become a certified animal trainer. Then, along the way, he'd bought the building that now housed his facility.

Often, he thought of the irony. Animals—dogs in particular—were his greatest love as a little boy. Had he listened to and followed his passion earlier in life, well... It didn't do much good to dwell on the past. He was happy in his job now and absolutely loved getting up for work every morning. He had what so many people wished for but never obtained: a beloved career that brought satisfaction and joy, and that also made it possible to pay the bills.

Isaac had started small, with just a website and cheap business cards, training pets in clients' homes, and eventually word of mouth spread and he'd hired on Hannah and Mike. Now they offered training at all levels from basic to specialized service, along with pet sitting and customized curricula for owners with individual needs.

At first he'd been reluctant to train dogs as companions for veterans with psychological struggles. The pain of Stephen's death was still too raw. But when a friend of his had returned home from war and requested Isaac's help to keep from drowning at the bottom of a bottle, he couldn't say no, and that aspect of his training programs had grown. Now, vets from all over Texas came to Friends with Fur to meet and train with dogs to take home and make their lives infinitely better.

Isaac's heart lifted each morning when he drove into

the parking lot, but it rose a little higher as he did that Saturday with the beautiful Avery Abbott by his side.

He hadn't specifically planned on convincing her to spend the day with him when he'd visited her home the morning before. But when he'd walked into Macy Abbott's kitchen, he was a goner. Avery's blond hair was wet from a shower and her skin glowed dewy fresh. He loved that she didn't need to fuss or put on a bunch of makeup; she was naturally beautiful, dressed in a fitted blue T-shirt, faded jeans and bright green flip-flops. When he'd sat down next to her at the table, the scent of apple shampoo from her freshly washed hair had filled his nostrils and made it damn hard not to draw closer to her as he'd focused on getting her to eat her breakfast.

He wasn't one to fall quick. Hell, he wasn't one to fall at all if the past was any indication. Aside from a couple of short-term college girlfriends and the nice-but-not-for-him dates the women in town set him up with, Isaac didn't have much of a romantic past to speak of. It wasn't that he didn't want love, no, it was more that he wasn't sure it was even possible to find what he wanted.

His mom and dad had been the perfect bad example of the kind of relationship he was looking for. He had to thank them for that. They'd taught him exactly what he did not want. What he did want was something simple, but right. Someone he could trust with every fiber of his being, someone who wasn't intimidated by the fact that he loved his work and that it was more than just a job and he'd have to put in long hours sometimes to make sure he got things done well. Someone who wanted to be a mom to his kids, and to help him raise them with good old-fashioned manners and sense.

Yet again, he thought, Avery brought all of this to the surface when he usually just ignored it and plugged along, happy to be single, but wishing for more. But what did he know about her, really? How could he even think of her that way when clearly all she wanted or needed was his help? It would be wrong to hope for more from her, wrong to show interest at a time when she was at her most vulnerable...wouldn't it?

"I've been by this place so many times," she said softly as he stopped the truck they'd borrowed from Tommy for the day, "but I always thought it was just a doggy day care or something. I didn't realize you were doing such important work in there."

Isaac smiled at the sound of her voice. As she unbuckled her seat belt, he snuck another good look at Avery over Jane's furry head between them. She looked refreshed after eating the blueberry muffin Macy had pushed on her as she'd left the house that morning, which he'd then insisted she finish, but he knew she'd probably done so more to prove that she could meet his challenge than to add weight to her thin figure. Oh well, he would take it, and if he had to spend every meal by her side that day to get her to eat, then so be it. She was his to take care of, at least for the day, and he meant to do just that.

He let Jane out and then opened Avery's door for her. She took his offered hand and he found great pleasure in the pink clouds that floated across her cheeks when their palms touched. Her beauty was quiet, like a landscape painting of a bright summer day. Makeup-free, it didn't demand attention, but once he'd laid eyes on her, he'd known he would miss her face if a day passed when he couldn't see it.

Isaac didn't want to think about what that meant.

For now, all he wanted was to spend time getting to know her better, helping her if he could.

"Oh, wow," Avery said as he unlocked the back door and led her into the building, Jane trotting happily along at their feet. "It's like doggy heaven."

She faced him with sparkling eyes and he laughed.

"Well, I'm glad you think so," he said. "That's exactly what it's supposed to be."

Showing the training facility to Avery gave Isaac the opportunity to view it with new eyes. He led her down a long hallway, showing her inside each of the different classrooms, stocked with supplies for all sorts of training exercises. There was a puppy room featuring long leads for recall training, toys and, of course, paper pads in case tiny bladders needed sudden relief, a large arena floored in Astroturf for agility training, and—Avery's favorite—the search-and-rescue classroom with its boxes labeled for different scents that would be filled and closed for dogs to identify. Finally, he took her past his office and up to the storefront, where his staff sold good pet supplies at discount prices, so clients could pick up what they needed on their way out after classes.

Seeing Avery's enjoyment of her personal tour gave him a burst of pride in the business he'd started.

"I love it," she said. "Very cool." She reached down to pet Jane who, Isaac noticed with a grin, had helped herself to a tennis ball from one of the classroom bins along the way.

"She has a mild rebellious streak in her, doesn't she?" Avery asked, teasing.

"Doesn't get it from me," Isaac said, thrilled when Avery let go a small rush of musical laughter. "But it's one of the things I love about Janie. She's loyal and reliable and obedient about ninety-nine percent of the time, so it just adds to her charm."

Avery stroked Jane while she listened to him talk.

"But damn, was she ever a mess when she found me. I suppose it was mutual, though," he said, his tone more serious than he'd planned. "I wasn't a very happy man at the time, and she'd just come from being a homeless puppy, so we both had some fixing to do before we were on good terms."

"And are you now?" Avery asked, her light blond eyebrows furrowed.

"Am I what?"

"You know," she said, as if he held the key to some mystery she didn't quite dare talk about. "Happy."

He stopped walking and turned to face her, thinking in silence for a moment, lost in the blue-gray storm clouds in her eyes.

"That's a complicated question, isn't it?"

"Not particularly," she challenged, a twinge of sorrow in her voice.

"Well, then, perhaps it's the answer that's complicated."

"Yes, maybe so, but I still want to know—are you happy, Isaac Meyer?"

.   In her question, Isaac sensed she was really asking something else—something along the lines of *Is it possible that I will ever be happy again?*—and he wanted, badly, for her to believe that, yes, she could be. Yes, despite everything that had happened to her, despite all the evil he could assume she'd witnessed, she could indeed find happiness again.

And, more important, she deserved to.

So he thought very carefully before responding, "Yes, most of the time, I am."

"And the others?"

He nodded. "Other times, I cling to the times that I am, and trust that if I'm patient, I'll find my way back to that place."

He looked down at Jane's happy dog face, remembering the days just after Stephen's death when he could barely breathe, let alone find the strength to drag his body out of bed to help his mother with her own grief.

"Sometimes happiness takes work," he said, ignoring the tension that came over Avery's body at his words. "Hear me out," he said, his voice firm. "We don't always want to do the work, the hard stuff, to put ourselves back together after something awful knocks us to pieces. But that's when it's most important to try, to keep doing the things we love and being with the people we love, until it meets us halfway. Some days, Avery, showing up and doing the work is enough."

He hadn't meant to say so much about how he'd handled his own pain after he lost his brother, and the liquid shimmering in her eyes hit him like a punch to the gut, but if his own experience could make hers even a fraction easier to bear, then it was worth pulling the stitches out of those wounds.

For her.

There was a great deal he would do to see this woman smile—this new, complex, damaged-but-not-destroyed woman who'd quite literally walked into his life.

He reached out and took her hand, glad when she only twitched a tiny bit at his touch before letting their palms fold together.

"There's someone I want you to meet."

Avery's shoulders rose a little and tension tightened her fingers around his; she didn't seem to realize how hard she was gripping him until he asked what was bothering her.

"I'm not... I don't really..."

"It's okay," Isaac said, running his thumb softly over the tips of Avery's fingers. Her eyes were huge, and even as he focused on how to calm her, he couldn't help but notice how their clear blue shade resembled the beautiful cloudless Texas sky above as they'd driven into town earlier. "It's just one of my trainers, Hannah, and a puppy we've been working with."

A smile spread across his lips involuntarily. "I think you'll really like him. He's a little fireball, but he's got all the makings of a great service dog, if we can match him to the right person."

She swallowed and some of the tension eased out of her grip.

"I think that person might be you, Avery."

"I'm just not sure if I'm up for meeting someone right now. It's been a few weeks since I've even—"

unmistakable embarrassment crossed her features "—well, since I've even left the farm, aside from wandering onto your land, of course. I'm just not sure if I can handle meeting a new person yet."

Though Avery's jaw was set with stubborn resolve, Isaac wanted to wrap his arms around her and tell her she had absolutely nothing to be ashamed of. He could see the scared girl behind the strong woman's facade, and his instinct was to protect her from any harm or pain, but he also knew from experience that she wouldn't get better by isolating herself from other people.

"Listen, Hannah works with combat veterans all the time, and she is one of the kindest, gentlest people I know. And I'll be right here, right by your side," he offered. "But if you want me to take you home, say the word and it's done. You don't have to do anything you're not comfortable with, Avery."

As he continued to hold her hand, Avery bit her lip, considering. Isaac gave her all the time in the world to decide if she was up for it and eventually, she pulled her hand from his and shook out her shoulders. "All right," she said, tossing him a confident grin as she rubbed her palms together. "Let's do this."

"Okay, then. That's my girl."

The words were out of his mouth before he could even think, and, slightly overwhelmed with what they implied, Isaac simply turned to lead the way back to Hannah's office near his own at the rear of the building.

But when he glanced over at Avery, he caught the

smile in her eyes and the way her lips curved slightly at their corners.

Just one of those smiles, he knew, could keep him going for a week.

Avery was out of practice.

It had been over a month since she'd met someone new, before she'd stumbled into Isaac, of course.

In her job as a nurse, she'd encountered new patients every single day, and for a time after returning from war, she'd managed not to let that intimidate her. But, as she had come to realize over the past few weeks, there were some things she didn't yet understand about her PTSD diagnosis, some things that reared their ugly heads when she least expected. Somehow, difficulty being around people she didn't know—and, more important, didn't know if she could trust—was one of those things. It didn't matter that logic wasn't involved; most citizens of sleepy, friendly Peach Leaf weren't out to ambush her in broad daylight. It was easy to rationalize, far more difficult to put into practice.

But, like Macy always said, she could fake it till she made it.

For some reason, she wanted Isaac to be proud of her, to feel comfortable introducing her to his staff and friends, so she would put on a brave face and try to keep her trepidation from reaching the surface.

He'd looked so happy when she agreed to meet Hannah and the puppy. It was adorable, really. How long had it been since someone had been so interested in her reaction to a new situation? How long had it been since someone had dared take her out in public and have her meet new people without worrying how she might behave? She couldn't tell if he just wasn't aware of how big a deal it was for her, or if he was doing this intentionally, to give her a chance to feel like a real person again, a person who could be okay in normal social situations. Either way, his thoughtfulness touched a place deep within her heart and somehow lent her courage.

Plus, if she were honest, she was absolutely dying to see the pup Isaac was so excited about. It was adorable the way his face lit up over a little furry guy. As far as Avery was concerned, a guy who loved animals already had a lot going for him. Maybe that was one of the reasons she found she could trust him so easily, even though they'd known each other for less time than it took her to binge-read a new historical romance series.

And goodness, how she loved the way her hand felt in his, and the way he'd grabbed it without making a big deal out of anything. He seemed to have an intuition for what would push her just beyond her comfort zone without making her feel pressure.

He was…wonderful.

They reached a door at the end of the hallway and Isaac knocked gently before slowly pushing it open. Jane rushed forward into what Avery assumed was Hannah's cozy office, stopping only when she reached a red-and-blue-plaid dog bed tucked into a corner. Avery yearned to see the little guy immediately, but she knew she needed to focus first on being polite to the woman who stood up from a desk and came forward to greet them, reaching out a hand.

"Hi, I'm Hannah. You must be Avery."

Avery shook Hannah's warm hand and, even though her heart raced a little, she was able to force herself to relax, knowing that Isaac was nearby and had her back.

"I am. It's nice to meet you, Hannah."

Hannah was petite with short brown hair, wide, lovely green eyes and an open smile that filled her heart-shaped face. If she was half as sweet as she looked, Avery could see why she'd be good at working with war-scarred veterans and dogs, and she could even imagine making a new friend.

"When Isaac texted to let me know you two were coming in this morning, I got so excited." Hannah squeezed her hands into fists at her sides and her enthusiasm for her work was palpable. "We've been working with Foggy for a few months now, and we know he'll be wonderful, but we just haven't found the right person to take him home yet."

Hannah and Isaac exchanged looks, but Avery was too interested in meeting the puppy to pay much attention.

"Can I meet him?" Avery asked.

"Of course!"

Hannah led the way over to where Jane had hightailed it upon entering the room. She stopped a few feet away from the doggie bed and called, "Foggy, come."

Seconds later, the cutest little thing Avery had ever seen came trotting out from behind Jane and plopped his bottom down right in front of Hannah, and Avery fell instantly in love.

Chapter Seven

When she thought of service dogs, a very specific picture came to mind for Avery, and that image was about as far-flung from the little furry bundle that trotted forward at Hannah's command as it could be. This was no regal Labrador retriever or German shepherd dog; no, this fuzzy creature looked more like he belonged on a greeting card or a bag of dog food than in a serious working situation. Granted, he wore a little blue vest that said SERVICE DOG in bold white lettering, but other than that, he could have passed as anyone's beloved family pet.

Avery's hand flew to her mouth to hold off the baby talk and cooing noises that threatened to escape against her will. She was an army medic, trained to keep a clear mind and to control her emotions even under the most extreme duress. So how could one little dog turn her insides to complete mush?

Unbelievable.

She had to touch him. The urge was fierce, automatic and impossible to resist.

Avery began to reach out her arms, but Hannah gently held up a hand to prevent her from doing so. The young dog halted immediately. Hannah turned up her palm, lifted it a few inches, and the dog sat quickly and quietly in front of the two women, waiting for his next move.

Avery's face must have registered her confusion because Hannah turned and gave her a reassuring smile. "We're just reinforcing how to politely greet humans. Foggy's doing wonderfully with all of the basics, and we've recently moved on to some more advanced commands. He'll make someone an excellent companion and helper."

Hannah beamed with pride at her little charge, whose tail slowly began to swish back and forth.

"Foggy?" Avery asked, and Hannah nodded.

"Because of his coloring."

"It suits him."

And it did. He was the cutest, scruffiest little mess she'd ever seen, with a coat of wiry fur in all possible shades of gray. Avery hadn't known there could be so many. His paws and forearms were snowy white, resulting in what looked for all the world like four little boots, and his tail appeared to have been pinned on as an afterthought, for it was long, thick and black as coal, mismatched from the rest of his little body. And his face—oh, that face—a large black nose surrounded by smoky whiskers, mustache and beard, dark-rimmed, huge brown eyes with long midnight lashes, and triangle-shaped ears that bent forward at their tips like little question marks. And her favorite part of all—bushy gray eyebrows that curved over and down into his eyes. It was a wonder he could see at all, but they were too cute to trim.

That face could thaw the iciest of hearts, Avery mused. This little bundle of innocent happiness was in stark contrast to all of the dark things she'd seen; it didn't make sense to her, in that moment, that humans could be so evil in a world that was home to creatures such as Foggy the dog. Her chest swelled and tightened and moisture poised behind her eyes.

"Yeah," Hannah whispered at her side. "I know, right?"

Avery couldn't speak without blubbering cutesy nonsense, so she simply nodded and stood staring for another long moment. When Hannah's tentative touch grazed her forearm, she jumped a little, then apologized.

"No, no—don't you do that," Hannah said, her voice laden with tenderness.

"Can I pet him?"

"Of course, darling. Go right ahead. Just hold your hand out like this—" Hannah squatted down and held out her hand, low, palm up, demonstrating "—so he can meet you."

Avery followed Hannah's lead and Foggy sniffed at her hand, his cold wet nose tickling her skin. Satisfied that they were now friends, he looked up at her with his giant eyes and wagged his tail at top speed. He spun in two quick circles and then showed her his good-boy sit again, offering up a paw.

Avery shook it and then laughed, covering her heart with a hand, feeling lighter than she had in ages. This happy little dog made joy surge inside her like a wave, and the foreignness of all that raw emotion—the sort she'd come in contact with so frequently since meeting Isaac—was almost too much to bear. She reached down and stroked Foggy's ears, slowly calming as she ran her fingers over their velvety fur. It was the same effect she'd experienced when she had pet Jane for the first time the week before, except, it seemed, even more special.

It occurred to her that this little guy could be her dog, and she could be his person, if he liked her as much as she already liked him, and if Isaac and Hannah agreed it was a good match. She might actually get the honor of being his dog mom, and, if Isaac was right, Foggy could help her with some of her PTSD symptoms; he could help her take care of herself a bit better.

They could take care of each other.

On top of that, she would have someone to look after, someone to love—someone who saw only Avery, not the bad stuff that had happened to her, not the mistakes she'd made or her bad calls, or the fact that it was her fault she had lost her best friend. Foggy wouldn't judge her the way people did, and he wasn't scared to be near her.

As she looked into his eyes and ran her hands along his sweet muzzle, she felt an instant bond that surpassed all logic, reason and science. It was like she knew they belonged together.

She ruffled the fur on Foggy's head and it stuck out in a thousand directions, making Avery and Hannah laugh. Then she tilted back on her heels and stood up, catching Isaac's gaze from a few feet away. What she found there nearly overwhelmed her. He looked so self-lessly pleased to see Avery getting along with the dog, it was as if his happiness and hopes for her were even bigger than her own.

He cared for her—it was written all over his face—and that scared the living daylights out of her.

The last non-family member Avery had cared for, had loved, was laid to rest in the Peach Leaf Cemetery.

She tore her eyes from Isaac and pushed aside Sophie's memory. Nothing she did could bring back her best friend; Avery would have to live with that for the rest of her days, but what she could do, what was in her power now, was to make sure something like that never happened again. And the best way to prevent someone she cared about from getting hurt was to keep her distance.

She decided then and there that she would let Isaac help her, and she would let herself spend time with him so that she could get better, so that she could be trusted again by her own family, so that she could get her life back together. And she would even allow herself to love this little dog. It was healthy to love, her therapist said, it was good for Avery to have reasons to get out of bed every day, but she would exercise extreme caution when it came to Isaac Meyer. She couldn't let him get too close. She'd already proven that she was dangerous, that for someone to risk loving her was potentially lethal, and she wouldn't let it happen again if she could help it.

What Isaac felt when he watched Avery meet Foggy was unlike anything he'd ever experienced before. In all of his years matching veterans with dogs, he'd seen plenty of compatibility and plenty of love grow from just a tiny mutual need for someone to care for. But this…this was something special. He could tell instantly that dog and woman were perfect for each other. Inside he breathed a sigh of relief, and when he exchanged glances with Hannah, he knew she was doing the same thing.

They had taken a chance on Foggy. Instead of the usual routine where they chose a puppy from a reputable breeder with a line of dogs of appropriate temperament, Foggy was an experiment, one that Isaac hoped with every ounce of his being would work out.

He caught Avery watching him out of the corner of his eye.

"Where did you find this little dude?" she asked, almost as if she'd picked up on his line of thought.

Isaac cleared his throat. "Foggy's from the local shelter."

"Oh," Avery said, not sounding surprised.

"Up until now, we've only worked with dogs raised specifically for therapy and service, but Hannah and I happened to visit the veterinarian a few months back to check on an injured cat she had found and taken in—she

adopted him when he was free to go after surgery—
and we met Foggy."

Isaac watched Avery, trying to decide how much
to tell her. Working with animals wasn't always easy;
heartbreaks happened now and then, and he didn't want
to cause her undue pain. At the same time, though,
Avery was tough, and if she was going to adopt Foggy,
she deserved to know as much about him as she could.

"He was unwanted and abused by his owner, whose
dog apparently wasn't spayed and had puppies with a
stray. The doctor found Foggy on his clinic doorstep
one morning along with his brothers and sisters, and he
fixed them all up. Luckily they all found good homes,
but Fogs was the last one and he was on his way to the
shelter that morning when Hannah and I showed up."

Avery listened intently, her beautiful face full of
emotion as she hung on to his every word, hungry for
knowledge about the dog, just like a new parent learning to take care of a baby. She would make an amazing
dog mom, Isaac thought again.

"It took him a little while to warm up to us, and then
we had to get him to trust us, which took even longer,
but from day one, he's been calm and easy, and, miracle
of miracles, he doesn't overreact to stimuli. He's got all
the makings of an awesome service companion. He's
just special, I guess, despite what's happened to him,
and we just couldn't bring ourselves to pass him up."

If Isaac could, he would take every animal home
with him from the shelter. They all deserved far better than the cards life had dealt them. And now that
he'd realized how much he could help them, he knew

it would be the very hardest part of his job to visit that place and have to select which ones to take with him.

Avery nodded.

"After we found him, Hannah and I decided that we only want to work with shelter dogs from now on. It'll take some extra legwork to make sure that we find dogs with the characteristics needed to do this job."

"What kinds of things do you look for?" she asked, bending back down to rub Foggy's back as the dog reveled in her undivided attention.

"Friendliness, confidence in lots of different situations and with different types of people, predictable, steady behavior, and—most important—temperament. Dogs, even ones who have been severely mistreated, can almost always be rehabilitated if people spend the time and effort necessary to do so, but they're not always good candidates to be service animals. For that, we need to make sure that we're choosing dogs who have never, and aren't likely to, display any kind of aggression."

"Makes sense," Avery said, standing up. "I think it's awesome that you're choosing to work with rescue dogs."

Isaac smiled, warmed by her encouragement. "It's not been easy to convince new clients that this is the right thing to do, but we're working on it. Every dog that we pull from the shelter that ends up being a good fit is more proof that this can work. We loved doing this before, but if we can save homeless dogs instead of creating a demand for new puppies, then it's better for everyone. We save them, and they save people. Everyone wins."

"And they do deserve a chance, don't they," Avery said. It wasn't a question, and she was so right.

"They absolutely do. Dogs don't ask too much of us. They want to be fed, sheltered, healthy and loved. It's not a lot. And so many of them love having a job to do. I'm not sure they understand it, but it gives them purpose, and if they're anything like me, that means the world."

Color drained from Avery's face and Isaac caught his mistake too late.

"Oh, Avery. I'm sorry. I didn't mean—"

"I know you didn't. It's okay. I don't want you walking on eggshells around me, Isaac. I need for you to tell me the truth and to speak openly and plainly to me always, even if no one else in my life will." She walked over and set her hand on his arm. "I'll find my purpose again, even if it's different than my nursing job."

"Yes," he agreed. "I have no doubt that you will, and Foggy and I will do everything we can to make sure that happens sooner rather than later."

A flush of color returned to her cheeks and Isaac felt a thousand times better. He clapped his hands against his thighs. "Ready to get to work?"

"Definitely. Where do we start?"

Hannah shoved closed a file-cabinet door and joined them, a manila folder in her hand with Foggy's name scrawled along the tab in thick blue marker. She looked back and forth at both of them, grinning, and for the very first time since he'd hired her, Isaac wished she wasn't so damn observant. Hannah was a very intelligent woman, but she also had a gift for reading people down to their very depths. It was a little eerie sometimes. And right now she had that look on her face—the one that told Isaac she knew exactly what he was thinking about Avery Abbott.

He was in trouble.

A little involuntary cough escaped and he purposefully averted his eyes from his very astute assistant, which only made her chuckle.

"I've got all of Foggy's records here," she said, coming shoulder to shoulder with Avery so she could share the papers. "I've been keeping a journal of our training sessions, and since he's been bunking with me at night, I've also got all of his basic care info, down to the last poop."

A totally ungraceful and absolutely adorable laugh burst out of Avery.

"You keep a…a *poop* schedule for him?"

Hannah, so accustomed to working with new pups, didn't get the humor. "Well, yeah, why wouldn't I?"

Avery giggled and Isaac couldn't help but join her.

"Hannah's very thorough," he said. "It's one of the many reasons I need her around here."

Understanding crossed her features. "Oh, yes. I keep meticulous records whenever we get someone new. Dogs need structure to be productive, just like folks do, so as soon as a little one arrives, I get him or her all set up on a food schedule and, well, you know, so we can make sure potty training goes…ahem…as smoothly as possible."

"Ha!" Isaac and Avery both chimed, and even Hannah had to laugh at that one.

"All right, all right." She poked Avery playfully. "You'll get used to it soon enough if you decide to join forces with this little ball of love."

She reached down and gave Foggy a treat from her pocket, which he gobbled up immediately.

Hannah caught Isaac's attention and got down to business, going over each task she and Foggy had practiced enough that the dog performed them consistently. The two had mastered *sit, down, come, stay,* dropping and leaving items alone, waiting patiently at doorways, walking on a leash, exits and entrances into vehicles and buildings, settling down on mats and crates, and—as Foggy had so awesomely demonstrated with Avery—greeting people with excellent canine manners.

Isaac could see that Hannah was as proud of the dog as she would be of her own child. He couldn't wait to get to work with Avery and Foggy.

Once he and Hannah had finished going over Foggy's training log, Hannah reminded Isaac that she had other things to do.

"I'll leave you to it," she said aloud, then, leaning in to Isaac's ear, she whispered, "Alone."

She winked at Isaac and it took all his resolve not to roll his eyes. Of course Hannah would know he didn't mean it and that her intuition about his budding feelings for Avery was spot-on, which would only make things worse. She knew him well and obviously loathed the fact that she herself had been happily wed to her high school sweetheart since graduation, yet couldn't inflict her own marital bliss on everyone around her.

He knew. She'd been trying for years.

"All right, Hannah Banana. That's enough from you now. I won't be requiring any further assistance."

He'd used his most serious voice, but Hannah only laughed and hit him in the arm with Foggy's file before holding it out so he could take it. She glared at him playfully before pulling her giant sunglasses down from their nest in her poofy curls and over her eyes.

"I'm off to check on the play area fence out back. Let me know if you guys need anything, you hear?"

"Will do," Avery called from where she'd been practicing high fives with a delighted Foggy.

Isaac waved to Hannah and went over to join them. He was a pretty content man before he'd met this woman, but seeing Avery having so much fun with her new friend pushed him right over the edge into full-blown happy.

She was beautiful when she let go of her shield and put on that radiant smile that brought light into her entire face. For a moment, all of the shadows were gone, and there was only sun. What made him even happier was that she looked at him that way, too. It was often easier, of course, for someone with her past to befriend an animal than a human. Humans weren't as simple or as pure. They came with baggage and history and a thousand secrets upon that first meeting.

Nevertheless, she'd let him come near her, physically and emotionally, the other night and that morning. He was so lucky, he knew, to have the privilege of getting to know her. He got the distinct feeling that she didn't let many people get even that close, so it made him feel special that she'd chosen him; he wouldn't take that lightly.

He looked forward to every second of their time together that day and dared to hope that there would be countless more to come.

Avery practically bounced back over to join him, Foggy at her heels.

"So, where do we start?" she asked, optimism lilting in her voice.

"At the top, of course," Isaac said, tucking a finger under her chin. He was rewarded with a sweet smile that reached all the way into those blue eyes he'd begun to like so much that his need for them bordered on becoming a craving. It struck him instantly and with great force that what he wanted to do in that moment was kiss her nose.

Chapter Eight

How ridiculous that his impulse was so sweet, so innocent, almost childlike in its purity and simplicity.

Most of his relationships with women—if they could be called that—up until that point had been casual dates that occasionally culminated in physical intimacy. Nothing serious, nothing complicated. He just hadn't met the right woman yet, to want more. He'd never felt a strong pull to get inside a woman's head, to know what made her heart set fire, what made her happy.

With Avery, already it was different. He wanted, no, needed, to know everything about her. He wanted to hear all the silly small stuff, like what her favorite movies were and what she liked to read. Was there something she loved to eat or drink? What were her thoughts on current events? What had she been like as a child? What did she want more than anything else in the world?

It was strange that he'd been so physically close to women before and yet had felt nothing like what he did when Avery was simply standing in the same room as he, breathing the same air. It scared him a little, yes, but he'd wanted to feel that way for so long that the fear did nothing to deter him from moving forward. It was too soon, he knew, to figure out whether or not this was what love felt like, but that didn't stop him from wondering.

It was certainly possible, wasn't it? It didn't matter that they'd only known each other for little more than a week, did it?

Isaac didn't think so. Life was short, and if something awesome came along and bit a man in the ass, it would be stupid to ignore it, to waste it. He had no intention of making that mistake.

"Everything okay?" Avery asked, and Isaac realized he'd been staring at her without blinking or breathing or doing any other normal thing to make him seem not kooky.

"Everything's great," he said, pulling in a breath.

Surely she couldn't read all the thoughts he'd just been having about her, about him, about the two of them. Surely she couldn't tell that he wanted to pull her close and bury his face in her golden hair, and much, much more. He studied her eyes, but they gave nothing away except obvious amusement.

"You sure?" she asked, tilting her head to the side, looking insanely cute.

"Absolutely." He cleared his throat.

Best get to work so his mind would have something to concentrate on other than Avery's lovely face.

"So, just a little info first. For dogs, trust is as important as it is for humans, although they're a lot quicker to give it away. For them, at least if they're raised from puppies, it's not so much that it has to be earned—although it did with Foggy at first, on account of his unfortunate past—as that you don't want to break it. If you show him that you'll reward good behavior, he'll give it to you consistently."

Avery nodded, her features registering discomfort at the subject of trust. Isaac knew it was something difficult for her, as it was for many people with PTSD. He knew it would always be something he'd have to work hard to show her if they were to build a relationship. That would bother a lot of men, he knew, but it didn't bother him. He was willing to work to earn Avery's trust. He would never break it if she offered it to him.

"And all dogs have something that motivates them."

"Like what?"

"Like toys, or affection, or food. You'll want to give all three of those things, but it's helpful to figure out what drives each specific pup. Foggy, for example—" the little guy's ears perked up at his name and he tilted his head to the left "—happens to love treats, so he's pretty easily motivated by food. Don't you, boy?"

Isaac dug a piece of dried chicken jerky out of his pocket and said, "Sit."

Foggy obeyed instantly, earning the bite.

"Very good boy," Isaac praised. He pulled more food

from his pocket and gestured for Avery to open her palm, then dropped it in. "Now you try."

Avery set her shoulders back and stood stiffly, almost as if she were at attention. Isaac smiled at her seriousness, but regarded her with great respect. She understood how important her relationship with Foggy could be, and he loved that about her.

"Sit," she said, then laughed immediately as Foggy just grinned at her. "Oh, geez," she said, turning pink. "He's already doing that, isn't he?"

Isaac burst out laughing. "I'm sorry, Ave. My fault. Let's get him to stand up first." Isaac winked at Avery before asking Foggy to stand. "Up," he said, satisfied when the dog promptly stood to face them, earning another treat.

Avery watched Isaac carefully as he showed her one more time how to request that Foggy sit down, holding out his palm the way Hannah had earlier, then lifting it slightly.

"You can either just say the word *sit* to get him to do so, or you can give him the hand signal. That way, you've got both a verbal command in case you're too far away for him to see, like in another room, for example, or, if you're in a place where you need to be quiet, you can give him the visual cue."

Avery smiled, obviously enjoying the lessons as much as Foggy clearly did. Isaac hadn't spent as much time around him as Hannah had, but he could tell already that the dog was alert, responsive and extremely calm. It didn't even seem to faze him at all that Jane was amusing herself by tossing a tennis ball up in the air and chasing it around the room as they worked. He would be an excellent companion for Avery, Isaac was certain.

"So, I can take him with me…anywhere?" Avery asked, obviously pleased at the idea.

"Oh, yeah, that's the whole point," Isaac reassured her. "He's got his practice vest now, which should let store owners and restaurants and such know that he's allowed to be there, and then he'll get his official vest when he takes his exam."

"Awesome," Avery said, her face lighting up. "I can't wait to see what my niece and nephew think of him."

For the next few hours, they practiced through several basic commands until Avery was completely at ease asking Foggy to do all sorts of things he'd need to know in order to move around comfortably in public. Isaac showed Avery how to let Foggy know that he was off duty by removing his vest, and he and Jane chased each other around the room, stopping at intervals to show their play bows and wrestle, while Isaac and Avery laughed themselves to tears.

Foggy and Avery were a natural fit, Isaac could plainly see, and they were already becoming fast friends. Plus, he couldn't help but notice how well Foggy and Jane got along, which was wonderful on the chance that, someday in the future…

He couldn't let that thought stretch too far. Avery was already warming up, even after only a couple of hours with her new bud, but he had to remind himself that he didn't know what she wanted. There was something between them that couldn't be denied, something palpable and solid, but he wouldn't push her.

Even if she was beginning to have feelings for him the way he most definitely was for her, she would need time to come to terms with what that meant. She'd been on her own for a long time now. She was a trained servicewoman and she hadn't depended on anyone except her fellow soldiers throughout her time in the military, and it was probably difficult for her to depend on her family now, so Isaac couldn't ask her to lean into him.

And yet…

What he could do was give her a safe place to be herself, to open up and start letting those deep, invisible wounds begin to heal.

The office door opened and Hannah poked her head through the door as Isaac turned.

"Hey, guys!" she called, pushing the door and walking into the room. "How's it going?"

"Going great," Avery answered, giving Hannah an easy smile. "Foggy is just…"

Avery looked up at the ceiling as if it might offer a word big enough to describe her feelings for her new sidekick, but then just shook her head and raised her hands in surrender.

"He's wonderful, isn't he?" Hannah offered.

"I can't get enough of him."

Hannah put her hands on her hips. "Has he been doing okay with all the basics?"

"Better than okay," Isaac said. "He's one hundred percent on everything. You did good, Hannah Banana."

Hannah shrugged. "It's my job."

"He's probably ready to take his test, but it'll be a

couple of weeks before I can get our usual guy out here to run the exam. I have no doubt he'll do great. And, if Avery's ready then, too, she can take it with him as his handler."

Avery bit her lip—a sign that she was a little nervous, Isaac had learned by making a study of her pretty face.

"We've got plenty of time," he said. "And there's absolutely no pressure on you at all."

Hannah sent him a look but he shook his head. He would bring up the subject of the local animal shelter's upcoming 5K walk/run fund-raiser when the time was right and ask her if she'd like to attend.

There were a couple of sponsors coming that word of mouth told him were interested in Isaac's new veterans program, and he'd hoped to run into, and if possible speak to, one in particular at the end of the walk that day. Having the owner of Palmer Motors offer to fund the program would be a dream come true—the money would make it possible to pull more dogs from the shelter to match up with veterans who couldn't afford to go through the training out of their own pockets.

Plus, it would be an excellent place for Avery to test things out with Foggy—all kinds of distractions would be present. But for now, she had had a long morning and was probably getting tired.

What they both needed was lunch. He wouldn't even pretend it wasn't an excuse for him to spend more time with her, to get to know her better, and he knew just the place.

"Well, guys," Hannah said, looking at her watch. "I've got to run." She pointed over her shoulder to the back of the building. "Isaac, the fence out back is fine. One of our new clients and his puppy are coming in later today to practice commands outside—" she raised her eyebrows at Avery "—and this little dude has a bit of a squirrel-chasing fetish. Had to make sure he won't get out of the play area and into the street. I'm determined to get him to focus, even with the little furry things jumping through the trees to tease him."

She winked and grabbed her purse from the file cabinet by her desk, then called to Foggy. "Are you coming, Fogs?"

Foggy stopped pawing at Jane and looked from Hannah to Isaac, then to Avery. He came to a decision and trotted confidently over to Avery's side, where he apparently intended to stay indefinitely.

"All right, then," Hannah said, feigning a bruised ego. "Point taken. Avery?" she asked. "Would it be okay if this little guy spent the night with you?"

Avery looked surprised, but then childlike pleasure took over. "Um, yeah, that would definitely be okay." She clasped her hands together in front of her chest, elated.

"Okay, it's settled," Hannah said, grinning at Isaac. "Let me grab his supplies. Next time you come in to train, I'll pull all of his veterinary records from the computer and print them out for you. He's been neutered and is up to date on all of his shots, of course, and he's had regular treatment for fleas and parasites. We use organic stuff as much as we can, and I'll be sure to give you a supply, you know—if things work out." She winked, obviously confident that they would.

Hannah set about piling up Foggy's leash, food and toys, then wished them both a good day and headed out.

Immediately, Avery rushed over and wrapped her arms around Isaac's waist, taking the breath straight from his body.

"Thank you," she said. "Thank you, thank you, thank you."

For a second, all he could do was stand there, speechless and unable to move. But then, when the woman didn't let go, he decided he would. Isaac put his hands on Avery's back slowly, tentatively, in case she decided she didn't want to be touched in return, but she didn't even flinch.

Finally, he wrapped her small form in his embrace and tucked his chin into her hair, feeling, for the first time, that he'd found his perfect fit.

"Well, hey there, stranger! I haven't seen you in years, honey, how have you been?" Barb's voice carried all the way across her popular diner as Avery, Isaac and Foggy—looking adorable in his service dog vest—stepped inside. Avery's stomach did a little nervous flip, but she took a deep breath and grasped Foggy's leash tighter as she steadied herself for what she knew would be a big hug and lots of chatter.

"Come here right now and give me a big hug, honey," Barb said, coming out from behind the front counter. Avery did her best to smile as Isaac tossed her a concerned look. On the way to grab lunch, they'd had a chance to talk about some of the things that Avery felt she struggled with the most, and she'd shared how her heart beat faster and her palms became sweaty whenever someone came too close to her. It wasn't so bad with people she knew well, but strangers were another thing altogether. She'd had plenty of panic attacks by now to know the signs, and he'd promised to spend the rest of the afternoon teaching Foggy how to block people from getting too near.

As Barb hurried over, Avery concentrated on the red vinyl bar stools and the black-and-white-checkered tiles that she'd seen so often when she'd waitressed for Barb part-time in high school. Focusing on the familiar setting soothed her, and as Barb wrapped her in a mama bear hug, Avery's pulse finally slowed back to normal.

"I'm so glad to see you, Avery," Barb said before turning to Isaac. "She was my best waitress of all time."

"You say that about all your waitresses," Avery teased, making both Barb and Isaac laugh. "You look fabulous, by the way—haven't aged a day." She meant every word. Her former boss's curly hair had a little more salt to balance out the pepper beautifully, and her blue eyes were as bright as they always had been.

Barb's cheeks took on a rosy hue even as she playfully swatted Avery with a kitchen towel.

"I'll let you girls catch up," Isaac said, squeezing Avery's shoulder before heading off to put in their order.

Barb and Avery sat at a table and caught up while Isaac waited for their food, and Barb gave Foggy plenty of compliments on his excellent behavior. When their order was up, Barb disappeared into the kitchen and returned with a baggie full of chicken scraps. "For Foggy," she said. "Don't worry, it's nothing fatty."

"Why don't you take a break and join us for lunch?" Avery suggested, thrilled at how pleased Barb seemed with the suggestion. "Macy and Tommy and the kids are coming by, too." She glanced at her watch. "They should be here to meet us any minute now."

Barb's eyes sparkled. "I'd love to."

Warmth spread through Avery's veins. Normally she wouldn't have asked anyone to join her for a meal, preferring the company of her family, the only people who wouldn't judge her, who were accustomed to her edginess. Then again, nothing about that day was normal, was it? She had a dog now, she thought, smiling as she looked down at Foggy, whose paws spread across her feet where he lay, and she had a new friend.

Perhaps more.

There had been a moment back at the training center with Isaac... She was certain he'd almost kissed her, or at least had wanted to, and the thought surprisingly didn't scare her. She would have let him. She would have loved it.

"There they are!"

Her niece's high-pitched squeal at the sight of Foggy pulled her from her thoughts and Avery looked up to see Macy, Tommy and the kids crowding through the front door, bringing happy noise with them to the table. She and Barb stood for hugs all around, and Tommy went to help Isaac carry over several trays of food. After Avery introduced everyone to Foggy, whom the kids adored, of course, it was quiet for a bit while they dug into Barb's amazing fried chicken, the only sound a moan of happiness here and there. And it didn't take long for the hungry kiddos to finish up and run off to the playscape out back.

"Hang on, wait for Mommy," Macy called after them. "I better follow those guys," she said, getting up from the table, but Barb put a hand on her shoulder and gently pushed her back into her chair.

"You stay here and spend time with your family. My staff's got everything taken care of, the lunch rush is winding down, and I need more time with those little ones. It's been a while since I got my kid fix." She smiled around the table before hurrying off behind Sylvia and Ben.

"What'd you two work on this morning?" Tommy asked before taking a sip of his iced tea. Only moments before, his plate had been piled so high Avery could barely see around it, yet Tommy was as thin and solid as a post from all the farm work. It was a tender reminder that he'd taken a rare afternoon off to spend time with her.

"Mostly basic commands," Avery said, smiling at Isaac.

"These two get along like peanut butter and jelly," Isaac chimed in. "I think they're going to be perfect for each other."

"Anything we can do to help?" Macy asked, setting down her fork to wipe her hands.

Isaac nodded to Avery so she could answer. "Actually, maybe so," she said, looking back to him for reassurance.

"We do need a third person for an exercise we talked about earlier," he said. "The idea is to teach Foggy how to act as a sort of barrier between Avery and anyone that might get too close for comfort, like a stranger in a store aisle or out in public, that sort of thing."

Macy and Tommy nodded, eager to help. Isaac stood and they all followed to an open space near their table. "You remember the sit and stay commands from earlier?" he asked.

"Sure do."

He smiled at her, his expression proud.

"It's just a step beyond that. So what you'll want to do is tell Foggy to sit and stay in front of you, but facing away from you. It's a little tricky at first, but you'll get it."

He showed Avery how to circle a treat around in her hand until Foggy was facing out from her front. It took a few tries, but Foggy was a great sport, and eventually they got it down and practiced several times to reinforce the move.

"All right, so now what we need to do is have one of you—" he waved at her brother "—Tommy, you'd be good since you're larger. Come up to Avery and stand a bit too close like you're in a crowded spot."

Tommy moved in, holding his arms out like a zombie, and they all burst into laughter when Foggy began barking at him.

"Thank you, Foggy, but that's enough," Isaac said, and Foggy quieted down, keeping a side eye on her oh-so-threatening, goofy brother. "See, he's already got the right idea," Isaac said, chuckling, "but we need to redirect it a little."

They spent the next several minutes practicing having Foggy stand in front of her to prevent Tommy from getting too near, applying the "block" command when he performed the move correctly, so the dog would have a clear indicator of what to do if a similar situation arose, like in a grocery store line or on a bus or plane. Isaac also showed her that she could just have her pup sit in front of her, facing her, so that she could focus on him as a barrier between her and anybody else while she did some grounding and breathing exercises to calm down. It wasn't long before they had it down pat, and Tommy and Macy had fallen in love with her new furry friend.

As they chatted happily, Avery took a moment to enjoy the sweet little family surrounding her, as well as Isaac and Foggy, and her heart swelled.

She'd missed so much, had spent so long in darkness that she hadn't been sure she would ever again see light. But this…this was a glimmer. It was like waking up from a long, fitful sleep.

She knew she still had such a long, long way to go. But she had to start somewhere, and, as she let herself soak in the enormity of the blessings surrounding her, she realized a simple afternoon spending time with the people she cared about the most was as good a place as any.

Chapter Nine

When they visited the park a week later, Avery had the strong sense that if Isaac and Foggy were not at her sides like two guards, she couldn't be sure that she wouldn't have just run away. The noises, colors, smells and all the chaotic stuff of life surrounded her as if she'd walked into a theme park on spring break opening day.

Gripping Isaac's large, steady hand in one of hers and Foggy's leash in the other, she closed her eyes and then opened them again, this time forcing herself to focus on one thing at a time.

There, beneath her feet, was the vibrant, soft Bermuda grass, a hardy green carpet formed from millions of thin, silky blades. She lifted her eyes and, straight ahead, they landed on the long, oval duck pond in the center of the park, gravel paths surrounding it like wagon wheel spokes. Above, the sky was the cobalt color of a robin's feathers, accented here and there with cottony clouds and glints of golden sunbeams. Several yards to her right, on the crest of a small hill, a young family enjoyed a picnic lunch consisting of what looked like chicken-salad sandwiches, dill-potato salad and spongy slices of pink strawberry cake adorning plates strewn across a red-and-white-gingham blanket.

The woman fed grapes to the small boy, who released peals of magic laughter each time she circled a plump purple orb round and round before popping it into his little round mouth, and a handsome man sat behind them, one hand at the small of the woman's back, the other capturing mother and child with his cell phone camera.

Down the path, an elderly couple strolled hand in hand, their papery fine skin linking them together as their matching silver hair reflected light from the sun's rays. College-aged men and women played a loud and happy game down at the tennis courts.

When she could pause and grant herself the patience required to take things in, one at a time, the barrage of anxiety that resulted from overstimulation subsided and the park was just a park, not a combat zone loaded with hidden dangers.

It was home.

This wasn't the place that had damaged her and turned her into a hypervigilant, fearful version of her former self. Instead, it was the one she'd fought for—imperfect, but full of hope and beauty—and freedom.

And, if she could only relearn to embrace it as her

own, retrain herself to know that it belonged to her, she could keep going.

She understood now, after months of therapy, that her PTSD would never go away; there was no cure for it. It would always be her silent enemy, lurking in the corners of her life like a predator, waiting for a weak moment to pounce and bring her down again. It would simply be a part of her forever. But hope wasn't lost, and she refused to focus on it, to give it strength. And she could develop the skills necessary for coping with the symptoms; she would survive. If she were lucky, she could even prevail.

Isaac's hand was on her shoulder then, its warmth reaching the skin through her T-shirt like a rich balm. "Okay there, sweetheart?" he asked, squeezing slightly.

Her lips curved upward at the buttery-smoothness of his voice and the term of endearment he'd used so casually.

"Yes, I am," she answered simply, not needing to say more.

Since they'd met, she and he had exchanged plenty of words, and talking and listening to him was, she found, a surprisingly welcome pleasure. But even more than that, she enjoyed their silences, those quiet moments of peaceful company, of just being together, that stretched out between them and required no dressing.

Now, though, she wanted to talk.

There was an itch in her chest and throat that she needed to scratch with words, with truth about the pain she'd suffered and had not, until now, had the courage to share with anyone—not even, if she were honest, herself.

It was time to open up.

She didn't care that the person she felt most comfortable with was someone she'd met only recently. If war had taught her anything good, it was that time was not the most valuable or the most important factor in a bond forged between two people. Rather, Avery thought, it was trust, which sometimes took years to build, yes, but could also be earned in mere moments, in small or large actions that communicated: *I am here for you; I will not abandon you.*

Isaac had given her that when he'd taken her into his home, fed her and offered sanctuary from her living nightmare. He'd done it by introducing her to Foggy, by intuiting that the dog would be a good companion for her and a protective layer between her and the world.

She could open her heart to this man, and if it bled, he would not startle at the droplets; he wouldn't run from her darkness. She didn't need months to know that much was true. She'd been given a gift in his kindness, in his generosity, and she was thankful.

Avery turned to face him and as she did, he cupped her face in the hand that had been resting on her shoulder. She closed her eyes, letting the heat of his skin seep into her cool cheek.

Wanting him to kiss her, to have him pull her near and cover her lips with his own, but knowing it wasn't yet time for that, Avery smiled and took his hand in her own, then led him across the grass to the duck pond. They sat together on the limestone wall that surrounded the pool of water. Foggy and Jane sat, too, at their feet, but their little doggie bottoms wriggled impatiently as they suppressed their urge to bark and chase the blue and green birds floating along the liquid surface.

"I never killed anyone over there," Avery said, her voice gravelly and so low she thought perhaps Isaac hadn't heard her.

He was silent for a full minute before responding, "You didn't have to tell me that."

Avery shook her head. "I did. I did have to tell you that." She turned and met his eyes. "It's what everyone wants to know, what everyone's thinking when they see me in town or talk about me behind my back, trying to figure out what happened to me over there. Sometimes, I wish they would just ask."

Isaac nodded. "Well, if it helps you to tell me, then I'm so glad you did. I'm glad you can trust me enough for that, though we haven't known each other long enough for me to expect it of you, and you never have to tell me any more than you feel comfortable with."

"I know that," she said. "It was my choice to tell you, and yes, it does help me to get that off my chest."

She looked out at the water and ran a finger over a long crack in the stone underneath her thigh. "I think people might believe I'm still human if they knew that about me. They might be less afraid to speak to me and say hello when they pass me on the street the way they used to, before I left and became someone else."

Avery could feel his gaze on her as she kept her eyes down, not sure if she wanted to look into his just then.

"You don't owe anyone any explanation, Avery. You

have the right to say or not say what you choose. And you did not become someone else. You may have added some terrible experiences to your résumé, but you are still Avery Abbott, and the people who love you know that."

"I'm not so sure sometimes, but I don't blame them, either."

"What makes you say that?"

"Just certain things have changed. At my job—my old job, I guess—for example. I was a great employee for years before I left, and I was thrilled when they wanted me back at the hospital after I came home. I was always at my best, always one hundred percent accurate in my diagnoses and medication calculations, often even more than the doctors I worked under. I never missed a day, I won awards and patients seemed to like me. Then, one day, something—I still have no idea what—triggered a flashback, and, well, you know how that looks. Anyway, after all of that time, I made one mistake and I lost everything. And I know that I scared the patient who was there when it happened. I can understand why they thought it best to put me on leave, but it still hurt."

She closed her eyes, remembering that tense, painful conversation with her boss. Avery couldn't help but feel betrayed.

"And with Tommy. The last time I had an episode like I did recently, he made it clear that if I couldn't get better, I couldn't stay in his home." The words caught in her throat and she struggled with the effort it took to say more.

"And the thing is, I don't blame him one bit—him or Macy. They have little ones to take care of, and if one of them had been awake, had come across my path when I was lost to reality, well—"

"Hey, hey," Isaac soothed, putting a hand over hers. Her fingers ceased their repetitive motion over the rock. "It's no good talking about what might have happened. The important thing is that your niece and nephew are fine, and what Tommy did was to protect them, yes, but it was also to protect you. Besides that, you are doing the work you have to do to get better. You're going to your therapy appointments, and now you've got Foggy and me to help."

She smiled at his sweetness, at his unfailing optimism. How wonderful it would be to have Isaac with her always, to lift her spirits each time they fell. But no matter how great he was, he couldn't fix her heart. She would have to do that herself.

"If Tommy really wanted to protect them, he should have tossed me out a long time ago."

"I disagree, and he and Macy would, too. They love you. They wanted you to realize how much pain you were truly in, and to help you find a way out. I just think they may not know the best way to do that. By giving you an ultimatum—a wake-up call, so to speak—they forced you to look for other options besides therapy. My brother was in therapy for a few years, and he still couldn't handle the symptoms. There is only so much doctors and medicine can do in certain cases. Sometimes you need a little something more, a little something off the beaten path."

It was Avery's turn to comfort Isaac. Lines creased his usually smooth forehead and his eyes were suddenly full of darkness she hadn't seen before.

"I didn't know you had a brother," she said carefully, not missing the past tense Isaac had used. "What was his name?"

Her statement seemed to pull him out of the depths of thought he'd been falling into, but the storminess remained in his face.

"His name was Stephen. He died when I was just out of college."

"Oh, Isaac," she said, resting her head on his shoulder. The gesture was meant to calm him, but it was possible that she'd benefitted the most from it. "I'm so very sorry for your loss."

"It was a very long time ago," he said.

"I'm not sure that matters, though, does it?"

"No, you're right. It doesn't. It still feels like he's going to walk back into the house and ask what's for dinner. And expect me to cook, of course. Stephen always was great at eating, terrible at preparing food."

He chuckled at the memory and Avery's heart picked up speed at the sound, glad he hadn't been pulled completely down into his sorrow.

"Do you mind my asking what happened to him?"

Isaac swallowed and tilted his head to the side, and for a second, Avery thought he might say that yes, he did mind.

"No, not at all. He took his own life when he was about the age I am now."

There was nothing she could say or do to express

how acutely she felt his pain, and she wished for all the world that she could take it away, that she could bring his brother back for him.

Isaac was the closest person she had to a friend since she'd returned from war, battered and bruised in invisible ways, and if she were honest with herself, she wanted more from him than just friendship. So it hurt that she had nothing to offer in the way of consolation. The only thing she could do was to be there, and be open, the way he was for her.

Isaac spoke, softly. "He was very sick, and I can't say that I was…surprised…but that didn't make it any easier on me, or on Mom. I did the best I could for her, afterward, but she was never the same. I think she lost a lot of herself when her first child passed, and even though I knew, always, that she loved me just as much, I couldn't replace him."

Isaac's jaw set hard and Avery could see the extent of his hurt, despite his attempt to rein it in.

"He fought hard, he really did, but it wasn't enough. His death is what spurred me on when I left my old job and started to look for something more important to do with my life. I wanted out of the office, big-time, but a lot of my motivation to do something more was my need to live life to its fullest—for Stephen. It was almost like I had a duty to live enough for both of us, since he didn't have the chance.

"He's what led me into working with service dogs. I knew there had to be something different for people who weren't making it with the usual medication and psychiatric help. It wasn't until Stephen that I came across research that supported what I always felt to be true about animals—that they can feel strong emotion and can even help us when we are overwhelmed with our own. They love us without judgment, even when we can't love ourselves and when we think no one around us can, either. They don't care where we've been or what we've done. They care only about the present, about living in the moment the best way possible. It's a beautiful thing and humans could certainly stand to take a cue from our animal friends sometimes."

"Was he—" Avery chose her words carefully, not wanting to press on any nerve endings or cause any more hurt than he already felt, but wanting to know more, because she cared deeply about the man next to her. "Did he serve in the military? In combat?"

"Yes, he did." Isaac looked up at her, and even though his eyes held sadness, they were also full of optimism, and she wondered how someone who'd been through something so difficult could maintain his humble generosity, his pure but somehow not naive, outlook on life.

"Is that why you help people like me?"

Isaac grinned and Avery's heart lifted, relieved to see that wonderful sight again.

"To answer your question—yes, Stephen is the big reason why I got into training dogs for vets. I don't want to see anyone in my community go through the same stuff that he did and believe that there is no way out, that there can't be life on the other side—full life."

After a long moment, he raised both palms to her face and stared straight into her eyes with more intensity than she'd seen up to that point. Flecks of gold danced around his irises as he gave her a crooked, perfect smile, and Avery noticed for the first time that he had adorable dimples in both cheeks.

Sparks of electric joy shot through her entire body.

"But I have to correct you," he said, suddenly quite serious.

She knew that this…this was the moment she'd wanted so badly only minutes before. Instinctively, she could feel that this was one of those times she would look back on someday with great happiness.

The moment she started to think she might be able to find it again, to find love.

Take a chance, a little voice inside her prodded.

"Why's that?" She bit her lip, nervous and elated, sad and hopeful, vulnerable and brave, all at once.

He smiled, his brown eyes glittering in the sunshine. "Because, Avery, you asked if I help people *like you* because of Stephen, when, in fact—there is no one like you."

He caught her smile in his lips as he gently pressed them into hers, kissing her with a delicious combination of tenderness and passion. She closed her eyes and let herself drop over the edge into something new, losing herself in the moment, enjoying the sensation of falling, falling, falling, with the knowledge that she was safer than ever before in Isaac Meyer's strong hands.

It was incredibly liberating to forget everything that had happened to her before that moment, every cut, every scar, every bruise that had pulled her further and further away from her true self, from the strong woman she knew was still inside somewhere, waiting to be set free. And she knew he couldn't do that for her. Only *she* could fight her demons, only she could push until she reached the other side of the horrors that she feared would always return in her nightmares.

She knew all of those things as she kissed him back, wrapping her arms around his firm torso. But she had to admit, it was mighty damn nice to have someone at her side while she did the hard work.

Kissing Avery was far more than everything Isaac thought it would be. He supposed they were still there in the park near the pond, with the dogs at their feet and sunshine soaking through their shirts, but at the moment, he wouldn't have been able to tell if his life depended on it.

Wrapped up in the sweet, honey taste of her lips, the ones that were definitely, incredibly, kissing him back, he lost all sense of reality, all sense of time, all sense of anything except *her*.

He didn't care that this was probably too soon, that it would mean things might change for them more quickly than either was prepared to handle.

It didn't matter.

This wasn't an ordinary girl, and this wasn't an ordinary relationship.

But there would be time for all of that later. Right now, all he wanted was to memorize the summery scent of her hair as its strands danced around her face in the gentle breeze, and the way her soft cheeks warmed under the touch of his fingers as they trailed along her jawline.

The way, when he'd finished kissing her, for now—
he'd already decided that there would be so much
more—Avery's blue eyes fluttered open as if coming
out of a dream. A very good dream.

As she covered his hands with her own and pulled
them gently away from her face, Isaac remained still,
mesmerized by her beauty.

"Kisses look so good on you," he said, not caring
that the words might be cheesy. Hadn't she told him that
she always wanted the truth from him, no matter what?
And it was the absolute truth. Her cheeks were rosy,
which only made her blue eyes shine a shade brighter,
and her lips were the color of strawberry jam, plump
from their collision with his.

She smiled and gazed down at their joined hands. It
didn't bother him that she didn't say anything. There
was no need to. Everything they needed to say had
already been stated in that kiss. The air buzzed between them with excitement and possibility, but they
had plenty of time to figure things out.

A loud growl interrupted the quiet and for a second,
Isaac thought it had come from one of the dogs.

"Someone's hungry," Avery said, laughing. She
reached over and poked Isaac in his abs. Not a vain
man, he was nonetheless glad he kept in shape, and her
touch so near his groin set his mind off on a path that
would be hard to come back from.

"Starved," he said, glad for the distraction.

He'd brought her to the park after their training session to relax and let the dogs out into the fresh air, but
the park also happened to be the home of a food truck

that served excellent burritos. The thought of lunch set Isaac's stomach to grumbling again.

"Let's do something about that, shall we?" Avery suggested, grabbing Foggy's leash and standing up.

Isaac did the same with Jane, but his girl wasn't a service dog, so it took a bit more work than just the "let's go" command to get Jane's mind off the ducks.

He'd kept an eye on Jane as they'd sat admiring the water. She had some hound in her, he was pretty sure, along with a thousand other things, and whenever she came across small animals her ears perked up and she fancied herself a hunting dog. Not that she was any threat. Whenever Jane got anywhere near a cat or a squirrel after a chase, she simply stood staring down her opponent, waiting to see if it would run off and start up their game again. She was completely harmless and a big doofus, but still, he always tried to make sure she was on her best behavior in public places.

"Come on, Jane," he said. "I promise I'll share some of my lunch with you if you'll promise me you won't run off after those ducks," he said, joking, but gripping her leash a little tighter all the same. At the mention of lunch, Jane's thoughts switched over to food and she finally decided that it was okay to leave the pond.

Isaac grabbed Avery's hand and they walked the hundred yards to where the food trucks parked. A row of shiny Airstream trailers, promising every variety of Texas cuisine, beckoned as they arrived at the gravel parking lot. Picnic benches painted in primary colors were scattered about, and kids ate rapidly melting ice-cream cones while their moms and dads munched on burgers and quesadillas.

"Wow," Avery said, her eyes wide at the sight. "I hadn't realized how much I missed this place until now."

Isaac shielded his eyes from the sun and smiled at her, glad that he'd picked a good place for their first date. Jane sniffed the ground, searching for dropped crumbs, and Foggy's nose twitched at the savory scents filling the air.

"We used to come here in high school," she said, her expression gone soft at the memories.

"Yeah, you were lucky to have it," he said.

"What? It wasn't here when you were at Peach Leaf High?"

"Nope. I'm a couple years ahead of you, according to Tommy. They built this right after I graduated."

She squinted, thinking about the timeline. "Oh yeah, you're right. It was my junior year when this all went up." She grinned. "I just remember sneaking over here on lunch break to grab hot dogs. We weren't supposed to go off campus until senior year," she said, giggling. "But you know, teenagers always follow the rules."

Isaac chuckled with her.

"So…you've asked Tommy about me, huh?"

Her voice was lighter than it had been before, and Isaac was almost certain it was more playful. His grin stretched from ear to ear when he realized suddenly that she was flirting with him.

"I have," he said, meeting her tone. Then he switched his voice to sound gruffer. "But, you know, I'm a professional and you're technically my client now."

He stopped walking and turned to face Avery, slipping a strand of hair behind her ear, enjoying the fact that he could touch her now without causing her to jump. "I make it a practice to know what I need to know about the people I'm working for."

"I see," she said, tucking a finger under her chin. "And what is it that you need to know about me, Mr. Meyer?"

There was genuine curiosity in her voice alongside the flirtatiousness. She wanted him to ask about her. This was the invitation he'd been waiting for.

"Everything," he said truthfully.

Chapter Ten

"I want to know everything about you, Avery Abbott," he said, staring into her eyes in the hope that she could fully recognize his sincerity.

She swallowed, appearing suddenly nervous.

Had he been too honest? Said too much? He retraced his steps, wishing he could put that carefree look back on her face.

"But first—lunch."

She relaxed, giving him a smile, and he reminded himself to take things slow. He hated the thought of going anything but full speed ahead now that he'd been around this woman enough to know he wanted more, more, more, but if he pushed too hard, he could lose her altogether, and that simply was not an option.

"Anything you want, sweetheart. Take your pick."

Avery crossed her arms over her chest and surveyed the selection. Isaac's favorite were the massive, over-stuffed delicacies from Freddy's Fajitas, but if pressed he'd have to admit that anything from any of the food trucks was guaranteed to be fantastic.

"I'm actually pretty darn hungry," Avery said, sounding surprised at herself.

"That's great news, and something we can definitely fix."

They must have been on the same wavelength because Avery's eyes wandered over to Freddy's and she headed in that direction. They ordered and walked away carrying giant tortillas stuffed to the gills with chicken, avocado, onion, sour cream and enough jalapeños to light the town on fire.

"A girl after my own heart," Isaac said, nodding at the spicy fillings spilling out of Avery's meal.

"Oh, don't get me started. I can't get enough. Macy is the only one who can make salsa that's hot enough for me, and I could beat the guys right out of my unit in pepper-eating contests. Every time."

She winked at him, proud, and he was thrilled to hear her sharing fun memories of her time in service.

"Man, I missed Tex-Mex while I was gone," she said, reminiscing and pulling her food a little closer to her as they walked over to a butter-yellow table and set down their cardboard boats of food, their drinks and a few paper napkins. Isaac excused himself and headed to the food truck to grab a plastic bowl, then took it over to a water fountain and brought it back to the table, placing it underneath for Jane and Foggy to share.

"How long were you over there? Afghanistan, right?" Isaac asked, watching her closely.

"Yep, that's right. Three tours, six months each."

"Wow. That's…a lot."

"It was," she said, nodding as she sat across from him and spread a napkin over her lap. "The time went by fast, in a way, but there were nights when I really, really wanted to be back in my bed, when I just wanted to be home again."

"I can only imagine."

"A lot of bad things happened, but…there were good times, too. At first it's hard, especially in Basic, because you don't know anyone and you miss home and everything is physically demanding and weird and it makes you all emotional."

She took a sip of her iced tea and peered into the distance, a trace of a smile crossing her lips as she watched a mom feeding a toddler little cut-up bites of pizza.

"And then, of course, you don't want to show everyone that you're emotional, so you try to hold it in and it just sort of comes out of you at random times."

Avery laughed at a memory. "Once, my friend Sophie and I were just chilling out after a drill, listening to the radio, and an old stupid song from the eighties came on. You know, one of those ridiculous, drama-queen hair band ballads, and I just completely lost it. I'm pretty sure Sophie thought I'd lost my marbles."

Isaac's chest tightened at the bittersweet picture she'd painted.

"Thank God I had Sophie with me over there. I don't know what I would have done without her." Avery's words came out a little squeaky and she hurried to tuck into her food.

They ate quietly for a while and Isaac relaxed into the silence. Jane and Foggy were lying under the table next to each other, their tongues hanging out.

They both took big bites of their fajitas and giggled as juice inevitably escaped to roll down their chins. Isaac pulled out a piece of chicken, wiped off the sauce and pretended to drop it under the table so that Jane could pick it up.

"Can you feed them people food?" Avery asked.

"Yeah, you can give them plain meat, particular veggies and fruit, eggs, stuff like that. Remind me later and I'll print you out a list of doggie no-nos. Certain things, like grapes and chocolate, are dangerous and potentially deadly to their systems, but there are quite a few things they can share with us."

He shook his head and gave Jane a look.

"I would not recommend feeding them from the table most of the time, though," he said. "It's hard to get them out of the habit of asking for scraps once you start. I've already ruined Jane for that. Foggy's so well-trained that you might be able to get away with it on occasion."

He pointed as Jane put on her very best sad face and rested her furry chin on his knee. "See what I mean?"

"Oh, goodness," Avery said, cooing. "She's too cute. How can you possibly resist her?"

"That's just it," he said, shrugging his shoulders. "I can't."

"I miss Sophie so much, sometimes," Avery said, so softly Isaac wasn't sure he'd heard her correctly.

"You were close, huh?" he asked.

Avery nodded, her lips forming a thin line.

"We grew up together and hung out all the time, but we weren't that close until we decided to join the army. I'd finished getting my RN at community college and was ready for a change, and, well, Sophie was tired of working low-paying jobs to get by. You know how Peach Leaf is," she said, glancing up at him. "Not a lot of work to go around."

He nodded in agreement. It was true. Lots of folks who were raised in their small town couldn't find well-paying jobs. The options were simple: go off and get a degree or other vocational training, or work for peanuts. Most people who left didn't come back, finding that they'd outgrown their hometown. Isaac could totally understand and had grown up telling himself he'd never come back except to visit Mom and Nana, but after he'd been gone a few years, he'd begun to miss something about this place. Even if it wasn't perfect, and hell, nowhere was, at least there were people in Peach Leaf who knew his past, who knew who he was down to his bones and knew what he'd come from and where he'd been. There was something solid, something important about a person's home. You might not always love it, and you sure as hell might not always like it, but home was home. He imagined Avery knew that very sentiment well.

"I do know," he said, giving her a soft smile.

"So Sophie and I decided to go big or…well…stay home." Avery grinned. "So that's what we picked. She didn't meet her husband until later, on one of our visits home, and then they had Connor a ways down the road."

"It must have been hard, being so young and leaving your family."

Avery shook her head. "Well, I don't know if Tommy's ever told you, but our parents were killed in a car crash when I was twenty-two and Tom was a bit older."

"God, I'm so sorry," Isaac said, putting down his fajita. He touched Avery's hand and she closed her eyes, evidently enjoying the touch he'd offered to soothe her. "You've been through so much for someone your age."

"That might be true, but you know, things could always be worse. I'm lucky to have Tommy and Macy and the kiddos, and this town, and I was lucky to have Sophie and to make it home in one piece. Or, you know, mostly."

Avery choked up a little.

"I just wish, sometimes—" she looked up at him under hooded eyes, as if choosing her words with caution "—sometimes I wish that Sophie had been the lucky one. That it had been she who made it home alive."

Isaac winced at her words and at the similarity they held to some of Stephen's later statements. He put down his food, suddenly not hungry anymore.

"Avery, please don't say things like that."

"I'm sorry, Isaac. I don't mean to be morbid, and I don't mean to sound like I'm not thankful to be here, but there are times when I think... I mean, I can't understand why it was me and not her."

She poked at her fajita with a fork, pushing around the contents that had escaped the flour tortilla.

"It's my fault, you know," she said. "It's my fault she's gone."

Avery's eyes glistened with moisture and Isaac reached over to stop her anxious fidgeting, covering her hands with his own.

"How can you think something like that?" he asked.

She looked up at him, her eyes huge and shiny and full of sorrow.

"Because it's true."

"Look, Avery. Whatever happened, whatever you think was your fault, please believe me that it wasn't. I know you."

Her brow furrowed and he could sense her skepticism.

"I know, we've only known each other for less than a month, but don't tell me that I can't feel your heart after that amount of time. You know there's something… something going on between us. Something special. And I don't need much time to be a good judge of character. And your character, Avery, it's the best."

She smiled sadly and he wondered if she didn't believe him. It would take more than words to convince her that what he felt was real and true.

"You wouldn't say that if you knew the whole story," she said, pulling her hands away from his to rub at her eyes.

"Then tell me. Tell me the whole story."

She closed her eyes and Isaac gave her the time she needed, taking a moment to check on Foggy and Jane under the table. The two dogs were snoozing side by side, their limbs and tails curled up, as though they knew they were meant to be together.

If only it were that simple with people.

If only he could convince Avery that he would be here for her, that he would support her as long as she would let him. That he wouldn't let what happened to Stephen, happen to her. He'd dedicated his life's work to ensuring that for as many men and women as he could help, but he hadn't known until Avery how much it really mattered that his program worked. It really could mean life or death for certain veterans. And those lives—lives that had been offered up in the most dangerous situations imaginable in an attempt to stand for the freedom of humanity—mattered. So much.

He looked up from under the table to check on Avery and noticed instantly that her expression was one of terror.

"Avery, what's wrong?" he asked.

The color had drained from her face and her skin was white as a ghost despite the afternoon heat, and her eyes were huge as she focused on something in the distance. Isaac followed her line of vision, but all he could see at the end was a man about his age, and a cute little boy who looked to be three or four years old.

Avery got up from the table as if in a trance, heading toward what he assumed were the dad and son.

"Avery. Avery?" he called after her, but she either ignored him or couldn't hear.

Isaac checked on the dogs again to make sure they were still asleep and hurried after her.

* * *

As soon as she'd seen them in the distance, Avery was pulled in their direction as if an invisible fishing line had begun to reel her in.

Nathan and Connor Harris.

Sophie's Nathan and Connor.

Her best friend's husband and son were sitting at a table enjoying a meal of their own, not too far from where she and Isaac had sat down to eat. Even from a distance, Avery could see lines on Nathan's young face that shouldn't have been there yet. He looked way too old for a man in his midthirties.

And it was Avery's fault.

She didn't know what she would say when she arrived at their table, which now seemed miles away as she trudged forward as if through mud. She just knew she had to see them, had to get close. She needed to make sure that they were okay.

Nathan had refused to speak to Avery at Sophie's funeral, and she couldn't blame him. She had decided that he agreed with her that it was her fault his wife, her best friend, was gone.

Nothing could convince her otherwise. It was her idea to trade shifts that day. It didn't matter why. It was her decision that had cost them all an amazing woman. How could Nathan—and even Connor, one day, when he became old enough to learn what happened to his beautiful mother—ever forgive her?

How could she ever forgive herself?

She neared the table and Nathan looked up, the smile that had covered his face as he watched Connor play with a fire truck evaporating when he saw who approached. He wiped his hands on his jeans and stood, covering the distance between them to meet Avery before she made it to where they sat.

"Avery," he greeted awkwardly, placing nervous hands in his pockets. She couldn't read his tone; it was absent of any emotion that might give her some clue as to how he felt upon seeing her.

Suddenly, she regretted coming over, wishing she'd opted to grab Isaac and run instead.

What had she been thinking?

They weren't exactly on decent terms. She had no right to just waltz up to Nathan like this and remind him of something he probably tried every minute of every day to forget. Just glimpsing her face probably brought back a million painful memories.

Suddenly, Isaac was at her side. She could feel him there as if he were a part of her own body, but for some reason she wasn't able to pull her attention from Nathan.

"It's been so long. I haven't seen you around town," Nathan said, his words shaky but not unkind. What had she thought he would do? Yell at her in a public place? It would be what she deserved.

"It's…good to see you, Nathan. How are you holding up?" The words burned her throat as they came out.

"I'm actually doing okay," he said. "Despite… everything." He tried to smile but it wouldn't quite take. "How about you, Avery?"

"The same," she said.

"How's your family? Tommy and Macy and the kids?"

Images flashed before her eyes of all of them gathered together, the Thanksgiving before her and Sophie's last tour. It was the last time she'd seen Sophie with her boys, and her heart ached at the memory; she was suddenly quite certain that her chest was going to explode.

"Nathan, I'm so sorry."

He held out his hands. "Don't say that, Avery. You know it won't help."

"But I am," she said, taking a step toward him.

Warmth spread through her lower back. Isaac's hand was there, holding her steady, but she couldn't look at him, afraid that she might cry if she did.

And she couldn't cry. Soldiers didn't cry. Tears were for release, to make people feel better. Avery wouldn't allow them.

She remembered when she and Sophie had first gone into that home to speak with a few of the local women who had gathered for tea. Avery's job was to check on them, to see if they needed any medical care or advice, to build trust so that they could later ask questions, draw information. Sophie, a fellow medic, was her partner.

They'd been surprised that day at how much they enjoyed spending time with those women—sweet, shy ladies who were apprehensive at first, but opened up over several weeks, eventually inviting Sophie and Avery to come by weekly. She and her best friend, using what little they'd learned of the local language and a lot of smiles, had established a repertoire with them, had almost come to trust them, though they both knew that was a very dangerous place to tread.

Avery felt the desert heat again, the dry, sandy air

surrounding her as she cared for an injured patient that morning, a soldier who had lost a leg to a daisy-chain IED only an hour before. She'd stayed late to prep him for emergency surgery and, when Sophie showed up to relieve her, had offered to extend her own shift so she could check on the progress of her patient.

Avery found out later that Sophie had decided to use the extra time to meet with the women, eager to get back early enough to take a Skype call from Nathan and Connor before picking up Avery's later shift. Sophie had taken another soldier with her, and they had both lost their lives when a bomb exploded inside the house where they met.

If Avery hadn't been so invested in working on that soldier that morning, if she'd just checked out and let Sophie work her regular shift, her best friend would be there now, sitting in the park with her husband and son, just as she should have been.

"Nathan, please. You have to know how sorry I am," she said, careful not to let her voice break.

"I can't do this, Avery. Not here, not with Connor."

She looked over Nathan's shoulder at the little boy. With his auburn hair, bright emerald eyes and a sprinkling of freckles like cinnamon across his button nose, he was the spitting image of his mother. Nathan must have seen her every day in their child.

"Can…can I see him? Can I talk to him?" she asked, folding her hands together at her waist.

Nathan's eyes narrowed and he averted his gaze from hers, his jaw clenched.

"I don't think that's a good idea, Avery. I'm sorry. I just don't think I can handle it right now."

She closed her eyes, willing the tears to stay put behind her eyes.

Isaac's voice came, low and soft. "Is everything all right, Avery?" He didn't bother introducing himself to Nathan. As it had been for the past couple of weeks, all of his attention and concern was focused on her. He was an amazing man, better than she deserved.

How could she let herself be so happy in his presence when her best friend was dead and it was all her fault? How could she allow herself joy when Sophie would never breathe again, would never again hold her little boy or see him graduate, get married?

Her stomach clenched. She couldn't.

Everything went blurry and she had to get out of there before she got lost again in the past.

"I'm so sorry, Nathan," she said, then turned and began to run.

She ran until she got to the duck pond and stopped, her breath coming in fits and starts as the panic threatened to return. She would never outrun it, could never escape it. It would always be there, lurking in the corners, ready to attack her at any second. She would never be safe again.

Her knees buckled beneath her at the reminder and she sat on the ground with a thud, curling her arms over her head as the tears broke free and spilled forth, dropping like rain into the dirt beneath her.

"Avery, sweetheart, it's okay. It's okay."

Isaac's arms were around her and he was rocking

her back and forth like a child. He sat next to her and pulled her into his lap, wrapping her up and soothing her, stroking and kissing her hair.

Safe in his embrace, she let the tears come again.

Foggy forced himself into her lap and curled into a ball, raising his head to lick away the moisture from her face and all of a sudden, Avery started laughing. And then she couldn't stop.

We must look ridiculous, she thought, *like a crazy, mismatched set of Russian nesting dolls.*

She laughed and laughed until her stomach hurt, knowing it was her body's weird way of reacting to all the pain that had surfaced when she'd seen Nathan. She wished he'd let her near Connor. All she wanted was to look into his little face and see Sophie again, just one more time.

But she understood. She didn't have the right to ask such a thing. Nathan had already suffered enough at Avery's hands.

Isaac's arms loosened and she felt his chin nestled between her shoulder and neck. She leaned back into his chest, savoring the feel of his strength against her back for just a moment. He didn't speak for a long time, just held her and let her cry softly.

"I'm a hot mess," she said finally, earning a little laugh from him.

"Everyone is, Avery. Everyone's a hot mess at some point in life. I don't think there are too many who make it out of here without some crap happening that breaks them apart for a while."

"Yes, but I'm the worst."

"No," he said, "you're not."

"How do you know?" she asked, turning so she could see his face just above her shoulder. She scratched behind Foggy's ears.

"I just do," he said. "But, Avery, you scared me back there."

"I'm sorry. That was Nathan. He's…"

"I know, I guessed. It's okay. You don't need to apologize. I just got worried. I thought he might be upsetting you and I didn't want you to be afraid."

She shook her head. "It's not that. I just misjudged the situation. I thought maybe enough time had passed that he would let me see Connor again. We all used to be so close and I miss that kid. He doesn't understand that his mom is gone, and to tell you the truth, I don't really, either, sometimes. I just thought if I could see him… I know it's crazy, but I thought… I thought for some reason that it might make me miss Sophie less. He looks so much like her."

Isaac nodded, his stubbly chin tickling her cheek.

"But Nathan's right not to let me near him. I've already done enough damage as it is."

"I don't think that's the case, Avery, but we don't have to talk about that right now if you don't want to."

She rested her head under his chin.

"What is it that you'd like to do? Right now?"

"I think I'd like to go home, if that's okay with you."

"Absolutely," Isaac said, standing up slowly and offering his hands to help her up. Foggy stood as well, waiting for one of the crazy humans to tell him what to do, while Jane bounced on the end of her leash, eyeing the duck pond in vain once again.

How strange, how incredible it was that she was now part of this little crew. How odd that she'd somehow taken up with a gorgeous, sweet man and two fuzzy mutts in a matter of less than a month.

And how beautiful, too.

Chapter Eleven

The sun was sinking lower into the western sky as Isaac pulled into his driveway in Tommy's old spare truck; his own had been towed to the shop and would be fixed within the next couple of days. Tommy had offered to accompany Isaac to pick it up when it was ready, but he'd already decided that, if it was safe for her to drive the short distance into town with him, he would rather have Avery's company.

She was asleep on the seat next to him and didn't wake even when he pulled to a stop. He let the dogs out but left Foggy's things in the truck so they wouldn't forget them whenever he dropped Avery off at her brother's house. When she'd said she wanted to go home, Isaac had assumed she meant Tommy's, but when he'd started to drive away from the park, she'd shyly asked if it was okay if they go to his house for a few hours instead. He hadn't asked why, glad that she'd wanted to spend more time with him, but he could guess that maybe she needed some time away from family, some peace and quiet to put herself back together after what had amounted to a long, tough day.

He'd texted Tommy and let him know he'd bring Avery by when she was ready, and to confirm that Foggy would have a permanent home with their family, something he and Avery had forgotten to discuss thus far. The kids would be thrilled to have him stay, Tommy had texted back, and he was happy that Avery would have a companion. She'd been lonely, he had said, and he was glad she and Isaac had happened upon each other.

Isaac didn't need Tommy's permission to hang around Avery; she was a grown woman and could make her own decisions, but it was great to have all the same. The two men were neighbors, and Isaac valued Tommy's friendship and opinion. Plus, he'd really enjoyed their fried chicken lunch the other day and liked the idea of becoming closer with the whole Abbott clan.

After unloading the truck, when the dogs were safe inside the house, Isaac headed back outside to gather Avery. When he opened the door, she was still sound asleep, her blond hair strewn across her shoulder like a scarf, eyes fluttering with dreams he hoped were happy ones. He pulled her arm over his shoulder and placed his hands beneath her back and knees, lifting her out of the passenger seat with minimal effort. Her head tilted in against his shoulder and her soft breath brushed against his chin as he carried her into the house and laid her on the couch.

The similarity to that first night didn't escape him, and he realized with a jolt how different things were now, how much more he knew about this woman who'd stumbled into his life.

How, even in such a short time, he couldn't imagine a day without her.

Nor did he want to.

He wanted her to be his—his to protect, his to take care of, his to…

Well, maybe it was too soon for that. It was crazy to be thinking about that already—or was it?

Of course it was. Avery was different from anyone he'd been with before. She needed more from him. Isaac didn't want to push things so far, too fast.

But then again, what if?

She was a powerfully sexy woman, after all, whether she knew it or not, and he wanted her more than he could stand to think about without sending his body into overdrive. With all of his strength, he pushed the thought aside, for now.

While Avery snoozed, Isaac took the dogs out back to do their business before setting up Foggy's bowl next to Jane's in the kitchen and filling them both with food. He checked that there was fresh water in the large bowl and, when the dogs were crunching away at their kibble, he grabbed a beer on his way out of the kitchen.

He'd expected to find Avery still sleeping, but when he got back to the living room, she was on the far side, staring at a collection of photos on the wall.

She turned to face him, hair falling onto the afghan she'd wrapped around her shoulders. "Is this your family?"

He nodded, holding the beer bottle out to Avery. She took a sip and handed it back to him. "Would you like one?" he asked.

"No, thanks. I'm careful with alcohol…with my meds and all. And I've seen too many of my friends spiral down with it, trying to medicate themselves." She shook the thought away. "I love a good brew now and then, but I don't want to take chances."

Isaac admired her. Like Avery, he knew many veterans—many people, really—who tried to find peace at the bottom of a bottle, but the end result was the same as if they'd been searching for a pot of gold at the end of a rainbow, and it would kill him to see something like that happen to Avery.

"That's just another thing that makes you strong, Avery," he said, reaching up to touch her hair. She closed her eyes as he ran his hand over her back and he pulled away, very much aware of the impulses coursing through his veins.

She was vulnerable, and he would not let anything happen that she might regret, just because her wounds were open and she'd had a trying day. If she wanted him as much as he wanted her—and God, he hoped she did—there would be plenty of time for that when she was ready.

"So," she said, opening her eyes and tilting her chin toward him. "Introduce me."

Isaac smiled and set his beer down on an end table.

"All right, but most of these are my nana's photos, so I take no responsibility for any stupid ones of me."

She laughed, the sound like a balm to his soul.

"So, this is Nana herself, as you might have guessed. She was an amazing woman—strong, smart, kind—like you." He touched Avery's cheek briefly, the gesture softening her blue eyes. "And this is me when I was a teenager."

"Very, very handsome," she said, winking at him over her shoulder. "Too bad we never had a chance to meet back then. I would have definitely been interested."

The breath disappeared from his lungs and Isaac sucked it back in, willing himself to calm down, to focus on something other than the beautiful woman standing right beside him, telling him she would have dated him if only they'd met years before, hoping that what he read between the lines was accurate.

He went on, desperate for a distraction from the sweet scent of her skin, from those berry lips he'd gotten to taste only hours ago, an action that had only served to make him want so, so much more. She was in his system now, he realized, and he needed another dose of her to keep him going.

"This is Mom," he said, pulling his eyes away to point at a faded snapshot of his mother holding a baby version of himself in her arms, three-year-old Stephen by her side, just after his father had left the three of them alone, choosing to start over and make another family instead.

Those had been hard times, with little money for a

woman with two growing boys to feed. It wasn't until high school that Stephen had been able to get a part-time summer job and help out; Mom hadn't allowed him to work during the school year, concerned that his studies would be neglected. He had then gone on to train as an electrician—work that seemed to make him happy.

Then 9/11 happened; Stephen was twenty-five, older than many of the people in his basic training, but Mom had been so proud.

Their lives would never be the same after that. If only it were possible to jump into that picture and warn them. Then his brother would still be alive, and he wouldn't feel so alone in the world, so rudderless without family.

Avery pointed to another photo, one of Stephen in his dress uniform, the red, white and blue of their country's flag forming a backdrop. "This is Stephen?" she asked, touching the photo gently through its glass cover.

"Yes," Isaac said, his voice breaking a little before he coughed and set it right. "My big brother."

Avery turned then and buried herself in Isaac's chest, wrapping her thin arms around his waist. He let her hold him for what seemed like hours. The world slipped away when she was that close to his body, and it took a herculean effort not to react to her touch.

He pulled back, not wanting to overwhelm her.

"It's okay, Isaac. I'm a big girl," she said, looking up at him with a hint of amusement.

"Avery, I... I don't want to push you into anything you aren't ready for. It's been a rough day and you're probably a little shaken up right now."

A tiny hint of annoyance flickered across her features and he hated even the idea that she might think he didn't want her.

"Trust me...if things weren't so volatile, if...if we'd known each other for longer and been on a couple of real dates at least, then this would be different."

She looked away and, though she still had her arms around his torso, tension had tightened her limbs.

"Hey," he said, urging her to face him by gently pulling her chin back until she met his eyes. "I want this. I definitely, definitely want this. But now isn't a good time."

She nodded. "You're right, Isaac. I don't want to go too fast, either." She said the words, but he detected a hint of doubt or disappointment in them—maybe both.

"We really haven't known each other all that long," he said.

Avery giggled, but then her face became serious. "The best weeks of my life."

Isaac started to speak but she put a finger to his lips. "I mean that," she said, and he believed her. "In spite of everything, and it has been a weird whirlwind, I mean it. Before the night we met, I didn't have Foggy, and I didn't have you, and I wouldn't change that for anything."

She rose up on her tiptoes and kissed him. This kiss was different from before—deeper and more intense. Avery opened her mouth and Isaac slipped his tongue gently inside, letting his arms slip farther down her back as he relished the honey flavor of her mouth, stroking along her teeth and the inside of her lips.

In seconds he was back on the edge, wanting her

with every cell in his body, lost in the wet heat of her mouth, all the while struggling to maintain some semblance of control.

He lifted her in his arms and carried her to the couch where they continued, hungry for more, but happy all the same just to be able to share kiss after kiss. He was careful with his hands, but couldn't keep himself from sliding them under her shirt, pressing his palms into the warm skin of her back. When she did the same to him, and just before he was certain all bets were off, he pulled away gently, settling her shirt back down as he placed a few more kisses on the tender skin beneath her ear.

Every inch of her body was on fire as Isaac's fingers danced over her flesh, and Avery cursed them both for agreeing not to go any further. At least not yet.

Now that she'd had a tiny sample of what Isaac Meyer could do to her, Avery's appetite was sparked.

He was right, of course, wasn't he? Maybe it was too soon for things to escalate any more, but that didn't mean it was easy to hold back. In fact, it was the hardest damn thing she'd ever done.

How long had it been since she'd been touched like this? How long since she'd last been with a man whose skin felt like lightning when it came in contact with hers?

Never, she thought. This was a first.

No one else had ever made her this desperate for more…of everything. More kisses, more touching, more time together. No one else could set her pulse racing with one look and send it into dangerous territory with a single kiss.

This was all new. This was something *more*.

As Isaac placed a few last kisses on her neck, sending tingles all the way down to her toes, Avery closed her eyes. He pulled away slowly, but immediately she wanted him back against her form, his heated skin soaking through her shirt the way it had been before.

"Ugh, you're torturing me on purpose," she said, her voice husky and full of thinly veiled desire.

"Trust me, I know the feeling," he said, and the gravelly, sexy sound of his words did nothing to calm her nerves.

"Would you like some tea?" he asked, changing the subject for both their sakes.

"I would, yes. Actually, if you don't mind, what I'd really like is to get cleaned up first."

"Anything you want." He gave her a sweet smile before getting up from the couch.

He headed down the hallway and a moment later, Avery heard him fiddling in the bathroom, followed by the sound of bathwater running. She hadn't even thought of that and assumed he'd just grab her some fresh towels and she'd shower. But a bath sounded much better.

Foggy and Jane bounded in from the kitchen.

"Hey, guys," Avery said, glad to see their sweet faces.

Isaac had fed them and they must have been playing together after they'd eaten. She patted the couch next to her and they both jumped up, happy when she covered them in pets, Avery laughing as they licked her face. When they settled down on either side of her, Foggy rested his muzzle in her lap and she scratched behind his ears, smiling when his eyelids lowered in pleasure.

Isaac padded back into the living room and handed her a steaming mug before sitting in the easy chair across from Avery and their dogs.

"I realized something earlier today. One thing we can do to help you out is teach Foggy how to get my attention if I'm near and you feel the symptoms of a panic attack coming on."

She nodded.

"I noticed that when you got too close to Nathan, you started to shake. And even if it wasn't him, even if it was just memories coming on too fast, I think it might help if Foggy had the ability to get me if I happen to be nearby."

"Yeah," she said, rehashing the incident in her mind. "That would be good."

She was quiet for a moment, looking down into her tea, thinking about all that had happened.

Isaac's brows knit. "I'm sorry I didn't get to you sooner. I wasn't completely sure what was going on until it was too late. I should have been there faster for you."

She took a sip of her tea, letting the smooth liquid warm her as she considered the apology she hadn't needed him to offer.

"It's not your fault at all, Isaac, and you know that. I just lost myself when I saw Connor's little face. He looks so much like his mother, it was like seeing her ghost."

"I can't even imagine, Avery. I'm so sorry you had to go through that."

She released a long sigh, pushing the air out slowly, trying to relieve some of the pressure that had built up inside of her over the course of the day. Isaac was correct; it had been a long one. And it was only the beginning—there would be so many more to go as she walked the road of recovery, able to see only a few feet in front of her, having to trust that the path wouldn't lead her back to where she'd started.

"Can I tell you something that I've never told anyone before? Something I would never say out loud to most people." She had to get this off of her chest for some reason. Maybe, maybe, she hoped, it would help. She knew she didn't deserve to let go of the guilt, but she wanted to see what someone else thought about something that had always puzzled her.

"Of course you can."

She twined her fingers together, making a little steeple as she'd done as a child, thinking about how best to share what had hidden so deep inside her mind for so long.

"I never... I never understood how she could leave him," she said, the words raw inside her throat. "How Sophie could leave Connor to go off to war, to a place she knew she might not come back from."

Isaac was silent, his expression void of even the slightest hint of judgment. She appreciated that he didn't try to find a solution to the situation, didn't try to make her feel better about it. He just let her say what she needed to say. Few men were like that. Few people were like that. And perhaps the world would be a friendlier place if more could find the patience and the discernment to know when to listen, when to let others release built-up toxins from their hearts without trying to ease the discomfort that resulted.

"I don't think I could have," she said. "And sometimes I can't decide if it was brave or..." She couldn't say the rest, but she knew he understood.

"When I left, I didn't leave anything behind except my brother, and he didn't need me to survive. I had no strings, and I wanted to serve my country, but I also wanted adventure. I wanted to get out of Peach Leaf and see something different than what I had every day of my life up to that point. But Sophie... Sophie had so much here at home."

Isaac let her words settle before speaking. "You were her very best friend, Avery. The two of you had so much history together. Do you think that maybe she did it for you? So you wouldn't have to go alone?"

Tears pooled behind her eyes. She hadn't ever heard anyone put it into such stark terms, in black and white, but maybe he was right.

A sob escaped. "That makes it so awful, doesn't it?"

Isaac got up from the chair and was at her side in an instant, his arms around her shoulders.

"It was her choice to make, Avery. She was a grown woman, and she made an impossible choice. It doesn't make her bad, and it doesn't make her good. It just is. It was her life and her decision to make, not yours."

He drew her into his arms.

"Don't you think she knew what she was doing,

sweetheart? Don't you think she weighed everything out? Just because she was a mother did not mean she had any less ambition than you, any less of a need to serve her country. It's possible she had more of a reason to go. What greater sacrifice could she have given her son than to fight to make his world a better place? To attempt to secure the freedom so many of us take for granted every day? And she obviously trusted that her husband and son would survive if something happened to her."

Everything he said was true, and somehow he was both completely honest, yet gentle at the same time, careful of her tender heart.

"You cannot blame her, and you cannot blame yourself. Neither of you knew what would happen that day when you traded shifts. And, someday, when her son is old enough, he will understand how brave his mother was, and how much she cared about his future, and when he does, you will need to be there for him. You will need to tell him how much you loved Sophie and how much he meant to her."

Avery nodded, wiping tears from her eyes with the palms of her hands. "I would if Nathan would let me. I don't understand why he won't."

Isaac rested his chin against her head. "Give him time," he said. "Give him time to understand that you just want to be there for them. He's mourning her, too, and everyone's grief takes on a different form.

"Okay?"

She closed her eyes, nodding. "Okay."

Sharing that with Isaac had lifted a ton from her

shoulders, and she felt like she could breathe again. His presence was healing her, a little at a time, in a way medicine and therapy had not been able to. She knew they were valuable, but being with someone who supported her unconditionally was worth just as much on her journey to recovery. She could see now that isolating herself from community hadn't been the best for her.

Now that she knew it was possible to find light at the other side of all that darkness, she began to hope that she might be able to repair other areas of her life, and maybe even get her job back someday.

Though, now that she considered it, she wasn't sure she wanted to go back to the same job. There was a time when it had felt like the only thing she ever wanted to do, but now that she'd been exposed to something new, she was beginning to think she might want to work with animals. She was a skilled health professional and had given much of herself to making other people better, but being in the company of Foggy and Jane had opened her up to something different, and she had the idea that she might enjoy caring for animals instead. Their presence was so soothing and full of so much joy. They didn't ask for much, just wanted to be treated with respect. It was something she could get used to.

"Now," Isaac said, getting up from the couch. He had to push a few dog limbs out of the way to disentangle himself from the wad. "Your bath is ready, my dear."

He reached out a palm and gave a little bow, making Avery laugh. When she offered him her hand, he helped her up and led her down the hall to the bathroom, making sure she had plenty of fresh towels and anything else she needed before he shut the door, leaving her alone with a tub full of fluffy, inviting suds. On the counter, she noticed, he had set out a T-shirt and sweatpants of his own for her to change into.

Cared for, calm and one hundred percent comfortable in this kind, generous man's home, Avery undressed and slid down into the perfectly warm water, her heart more at ease than it had been since she could remember.

But only a few moments passed before she wanted him back by her side.

She was ready now, to have everything.

"Isaac?" she called.

She heard his footsteps coming closer down the hall and then they stopped just outside the door.

"What is it?"

"I need one more thing," she said, gripping the sides of the tub to lift herself from the warm water.

"Anything. Just say the word." His voice, so near, yet so distant, on the other side of the door, vibrated up her spine.

She bit her lower lip to keep from grinning like a madwoman, to quell the raging desire growing swiftly in the most neglected parts of her body. Drawing in a deep breath, she headed for the door, slowly opening it until she stood completely bare before him. His dark eyes said far more than any words might have as they took in the whole of her form. She'd already given him her heart; now she wanted him to have all of her.

"I need you."

She didn't have to say another word. He gave her the sultriest smile she'd ever witnessed and, within seconds, he'd wrapped his arms around her naked body and carried her, dripping wet, down the hallway to his bedroom, closing the door behind them.

The only light in the room came from the last soft rays of evening sun that slipped in through Isaac's window, but his eyes seemed to be on fire as he laid her gently on the bed, taking a moment to drink in the sight of her once more.

She felt no shyness under his gaze, only raw need as he tugged off his shirt and came closer to the side of the bed, to her. She lifted her torso and wrapped her arms around his waist, hugging him tightly before she let go and slid her fingers up to the waistband of his jeans.

But then he pulled her hands away and lowered himself until he was eye level with her. "Avery, are you sure this is what you want?" he asked, his breath halting over the words, forehead knit with concern. Her insides ached at the knowledge of what she was doing to him, and at how much he respected her boundaries. But that was just it—she wanted no more boundaries between them.

"Absolutely," she said, drawing his mouth to hers as she threaded her fingers through that thick, unruly, dark hair she loved so much. Then his palms were against her cheeks, his thumbs tracing over her face as the kiss deepened, further and further until both of them needed something far more intense.

Isaac rose again and, this time, made no move to stop her undoing his jeans. When they fell to the floor in a heap, leaving only the stark outline of his desire for her against the taut material of his boxer briefs, it was her turn to study him unbridled.

And study him, she did.

He was incredible in every way possible, this man who loved her, and she wanted him more than anything else in the world.

Resting her hands on his waist, she pulled him down to join her on the bed.

"We can go slow. There's no rush, you know." She heard the words, but they didn't sound too convincing.

"Actually," she said, giggling as she admired the view of him hovering above her, "I am in a rush." His brows rose in confusion, but she went on. "It's taken my whole life to find the perfect guy for me, and now that I have you, I'm totally ready to dive in."

His head leaned back and he laughed, the warm sound affecting her almost as much as the hands that soon covered her breasts. With her, all their clothes and inhibitions now gone, he was wilder and more sensual than any of the rogues and rakes that populated her favorite novels. And it occurred to her suddenly, she was the lucky heroine who got to belong to him, to be the one he placed above all others, the one he fought for and rode off with into the sunset.

"Well, in that case…"

He leaned down to kiss her flesh, moving one hand to stroke the heated center of her, eliciting a moan so primal she wasn't even sure it was she who'd uttered it.

As he drove her to the edge of sanity, she reached out to hold him, drawing his aroused body closer to her own until neither of them could stand to wait any longer, and Isaac paused briefly to get a condom from his bedside table. Their breath came in heavy waves, skin burning with hunger for each other as their mouths met again. And when he finally crashed into her, filling every empty space inside, Avery let go completely and gave him everything she had.

Hours later, Avery stirred in a fitful sleep, tossing her arms and legs as she struggled against another horrifying nightmare.

In the dream, she and Sophie were together again. Instead of trading shifts, they had gone to visit some of the Afghan women at their normal time. The sun was high in the desert sky as they made their way down the dirt street to the home, and their hearts were lighter than usual. The rays beat down but their skin was protected from the worst of it by the burkas they wore with their uniforms.

The house was quiet as the two women were invited in, welcomed warmly and given tea as usual, but something was different. There was a new woman amidst them, one they hadn't met before who seemed to stare at them with apprehension, and something more. Something like thinly veiled hatred.

Tension buzzed and the air was thick with electricity, as just before a storm. Avery sensed that they shouldn't linger, and she finished her refreshments quickly before suggesting to Sophie that they ask if any of the women needed any medical help and then return quickly to their turf, where they would be relatively safe.

Even as she slept, Avery knew how the dream would

end. She knew there would be nothing she could do to stop the bomb from going off while she and Sophie remained in the house. She didn't know why she was with her friend in the dream when she had not been in real life; perhaps on some level it was what she wanted subconsciously, what she wished had happened so that they would both be gone and she wouldn't be home, alone, living with too-heavy guilt in a place where no one understood what she did.

But this time, as she braced herself for the blast, something changed.

When she reached up to touch her face, instead of sand there was moisture, and…something warm. Confusion set in as her eyes fluttered open, and there he was. There was Foggy, his paws near her shoulders as he licked her cheeks with vigor, willing her to wake up and see that she was okay. She wasn't in that desert like she'd been the last time she'd had that nightmare.

Though this time, it didn't take long for her to remember that she was in Isaac's home—that in fact she lay next to him in his own bed. After several hours together the evening before, they'd opened the door and let the dogs pile up at the foot of the king-size bed. Sensing her distress even as she dreamed, Foggy must have crawled to her side.

Coming to, she buried her fingers in the fur just behind Foggy's shoulders and pulled his head close, hugging him for dear life, realizing with elation that he'd woken her up on purpose. He'd saved her from the worst part of the dream. He reminded her what was real.

She put her hands on the sides of his face and planted

a giant kiss on his cold, wet nose. "You wonderful little dog," she said, sitting up in bed and reaching around to hug him some more. "You amazing little creature."

Tears began to spill down her cheeks as she understood fully what Foggy had done for her. She held him close for a long time, starting only when she felt Isaac's hand on her shoulder.

"Hey there, handsome," she said, wiping at her eyes with the palms of her hands, as laughter welled up inside.

Isaac sat up and scooted closer to her side of the bed. As she turned to him, her eyes slid over the hard planes of his chest and abs, then back up to his gorgeously stubbled face. His dark hair stuck out all over the place and she wanted to run her fingers through it and mess it up even more.

"Come here," she said again, and Isaac scooted even closer, snuggling her against his chest and burying his sleepy face into her hair.

"Is everything okay? I think I heard you crying but it took me a minute to fully wake up."

"Yes, it's okay," she said, giggling now between little happy sobs. Images filled her mind of him kissing her good-night a few hours before, just after they'd made love for the countless time, bringing a glass of water to place at her bedside table. He'd made sure she had everything she needed to be comfortable in his home before he crawled under the sheets by her side, both of them happily exhausted.

"What happened? Did you have another nightmare?"

She nodded and Isaac's hand landed on her thigh,

warm even through the sheets. "But it's all right this time."

Isaac looked confused and she pointed at the dog in her arms.

"It's all right, because this time, Foggy saved me."

Chapter Twelve

"Avery, I'm so very glad to see you," Dr. Santiago greeted as Avery opened her office door at the Veterans Affairs outpatient clinic the next Thursday, right on time for her one o'clock appointment.

The doctor stood and shook Avery's hand, welcoming her with a broad, sincere smile. "I always look forward to our appointments. Would you like something to drink today? I have the usual Coke and water."

Avery tilted her head and chewed her lip. "I'll have a Coke today, if you don't mind."

Dr. Santiago paused in front of the minifridge in the corner behind her long, oak desk. "Special occasion?" she joked, and Avery smiled.

"No. Just feeling adventurous, I guess."

"Well, by all means. Coke it is." She pulled out a

can and handed it across her workspace before sitting down. Avery gripped the ice-cold drink and flipped open the tab to take a sip. It had been ages since she'd had a Coke and she'd forgotten how much she enjoyed the sugary, caramely soda.

"My goodness, this is good," she accidentally said out loud.

Dr. Santiago grinned as Avery took the seat across from her. "I'm so glad you like it. It's good to see you indulging a little."

They had spoken before about Avery's diminished appetite and low body weight, but the doctor had always been kind and gentle, urging her patient to speak about why it was difficult for her to eat, sometimes even having Avery list the things she used to enjoy eating in the hopes of encouraging her hunger to perk back up, so she wasn't surprised at the comment.

"It feels good to enjoy something like this again, even something so insignificant."

"Or maybe not so insignificant," Dr. Santiago suggested. "Sometimes it's the littlest things that give us something to cling to, almost like a breadcrumb to help you find your way back."

Dr. Santiago was tall, with silky black hair and matching eyes, and a deep but soft, soothing voice infused with a native Puerto Rican Spanish accent. She was Avery's favorite therapist, the only one she had been able to commit to seeing on a regular basis. Some of the others had cold, overly bright offices and demeanors that Avery's body actively resisted, making it impossible for her to relax or trust them, but Dr. Santiago had decorated her space in peaceful deep purples and soft greens. The velvety indigo couch Avery now sat on was overstuffed and comfortable, situated directly across from a gorgeous print of the Sangre de Cristo Mountains.

The picture reminded Avery of their first consultation. She'd asked Dr. Santiago if she had ever been to those mountains, and, unlike most of the doctors Avery had visited, this one did not try to avoid the question and redirect her back to the horrors of her own mind. Instead, Dr. Santiago had offered Avery a warm smile and answered, telling of her annual trips there, of the solace she found hiking those foothills with the little terrier that was her constant companion.

Avery considered what the doctor had said about breadcrumbs and trails. "I think I may have found another breadcrumb."

"Oh?"

Avery's lips turned up involuntarily and she hoped she wasn't blushing like a little girl. "I met someone recently…someone very interesting, very different and incredibly sweet. Isaac."

Dr. Santiago leaned forward, and for a moment Avery recalled what it was like to share something exciting with a close girlfriend. She hadn't realized until that moment how much she missed female companionship. Macy was wonderful, but it wasn't often that the two of them were alone without the kids. She should remedy that, Avery thought, and suggest that Macy join her for a drink sometime, out of the house, away from all the everyday stuff. There was a time when going out like that had been a weekly Friday thing, something she looked forward to.

Why had they stopped?

Because of me, Avery thought. Her friends and sister-in-law probably didn't know what to say to get those girls' nights out started up again. Her impulse was to blame them, but Avery knew it was just as much on her end. Maybe they could reach out to her a little more, but she hadn't exactly been outgoing lately. She could stand to make more of an effort, and maybe they would meet her in the middle. Her friends loved her, she knew. They had come by in droves after she'd come home, bringing flowers and magazines and the romance novels she loved, treating her like she might be sick.

And she was. But there was no medicine that could make her wholly better. And she'd thanked them, but eventually pushed them all away, as much afraid of them as they were of her. She realized that now, the same as she realized she needed them.

Maybe they *were* the medicine. Her friends, and Foggy, and Isaac, and her family. She could hold on to them if she wanted to, if she could let herself be that vulnerable, and they would be her borrowed strength until she built enough of her own to stand up again.

"Avery?"

"Hmm?"

"If you want to share, I'd love to hear more about Isaac."

"Oh, yes, Isaac." She let his name linger on her lips, enjoying the soft symmetry of its syllables. "Isaac."

Dr. Santiago smiled.

"He's a certified dog trainer, actually, who also happens to be my brother's neighbor. Oddly enough, even though he lives literally just up the road, I only met him a few weeks ago, and I've been spending almost all of my time with him since." She paused at the memory, thinking of how a bad situation turned so quickly, so unexpectedly, into something good.

"I was having one of my flashback episodes," she said, looking up to meet Dr. Santiago's eyes. They were concerned but nonjudgmental, full of kindness and understanding, much like those of the man she was describing.

"He found me, or I found him, and he took me home, fed me and took care of me. I was terrified when I realized what had happened, but he was so wonderful with me, so patient and compassionate when I told him what was going on. Then, when I found out that he works with service dogs for veterans with PTSD, it was almost like…like it was meant to be, even though I don't really believe in that nonsense. I can't explain the way I feel around him—it's something completely new to me."

Dr. Santiago nodded, urging Avery to go on.

"He took me to his training facility the next week and introduced me to a dog that he'd been working with. They hadn't found a person for him yet, so Isaac asked if I might be interested in training with the dog—Foggy—and of course I was. I've always loved dogs. We've been working together a little bit every day, and Isaac and I have been on a couple of wonderful dates. This weekend, we're going to the 5K walk/run for the local animal shelter. It'll be a good place for Foggy and

I to practice being around a bunch of people and dogs at the same time, plus a lot of other stimulation, though I have no doubt we'll do wonderfully."

"That sounds marvelous, Avery. I'm so very happy for you."

"It is. It is marvelous. I feel so lucky, you know. Sometimes it takes ages for people who need them to get service dogs, yet this one just sort of fell into my lap and I have no idea why."

"Who knows why? But this is a good thing for you, Avery. I'm giving you full permission to enjoy it. In fact, that's my medical advice for you in this situation. Enjoy it to the fullest."

Avery laughed, but she did let the doctor's words sink in. "I'm just not sure I deserve something so amazing."

"Oh, but you do. I cannot convince you of that— it's something we've talked about previously and it's something you know you'll have to come to embrace on your own—but you very much do deserve good things in life."

Avery nodded, trying hard not to argue with what, on some level she hadn't yet acknowledged, she knew to be the truth.

"Another thing—I've seen this many times—your insurance may or may not have covered a service animal if you had sought one on your own and put in a claim, and in my experience, they can cost twenty-thousand dollars or more. In this field, we are just beginning to understand how valuable these interspecies relationships can be, and we know almost without a doubt that dogs, horses and even other animals can serve as excellent helpers with victims of psychological trauma, but we've only scratched the surface of compiling enough solid research to convince the insurance companies of the numerous benefits."

Avery's eyes widened at the amount. She had never even thought about getting a dog to help with her PTSD. Not until she'd met Isaac. But now, now that she'd met Foggy and spent time with him, she could see his incredible value, and she knew firsthand that it took a long time and a lot of funding to train a service dog. More important, she missed him every second he was away from her, almost as much as she did Isaac. Even then, as the two guys waited for her in the lobby, she had a hard time fathoming her life without either. She needed them. It was a huge sign of weakness, of vulnerability, to need them, she knew. But it was also completely normal. It was human.

"So, in my opinion, based on what you've told me, it sounds like you've stumbled upon a very favorable situation."

Avery beamed. She hadn't known she'd wanted Dr. Santiago's advice, but now that she had it, she felt even better. She knew, and her doctor knew, that she wasn't one to jump headfirst into things that she wasn't 100 percent confident about. It was a leap of faith to choose to trust Isaac, and even though she was still skeptical that any person could be trusted, she knew he was worthy.

"Thank you, Dr. Santiago. That means a lot to me."

"You like him very much, don't you?"

"Yes, very much. In fact, I think I might even be falling in love with him."

"I haven't seen you looking this well or thinking this positively since we met, you know."

"I know."

Sensing that their session was drawing close to the end of its allotted hour, Avery pulled her cell phone out of the pocket of her jeans and slipped her finger across the screen to wake it up. Sure enough, it was almost time for her to go. She usually hated leaving these appointments, knowing that her world would be unsteady until the next one, that she'd miss Dr. Santiago's sanctuary of an office and the woman herself more than was possibly healthy. But today was different. Today, she had time with Isaac and Foggy to look forward to. They were waiting outside the door. For her. And she couldn't wait to see them again and to find out what Isaac had in store for their afternoon.

Their dates were always so much better than just going out to dinner, though they had done plenty of that, as well. So far, Isaac had taken her to pick fresh peaches at the orchards of their town's namesake, which they'd taken home and baked into an incredible cobbler. They'd been boating at the lake, window-shopping downtown, to the dog park and to a movie at the local outdoor drive-in. Each day and night with him was like a new adventure, and even when they just stayed in and hung out together, she was happier than she'd ever been in her life.

She checked the time and put her phone away.

"Okay, for homework—which I already know you

don't like—I want you to write down five things that make you happy."

It took concentrated effort for Avery to restrain her reaction to this week's assignment, but she had to laugh at how well the psychiatrist knew her patient.

It wouldn't hurt to be more open. After all, look how much good had happened once she'd chosen to open her heart to Isaac.

"All right, and then what do I do with the list?"

Dr. Santiago took a sip of the peppermint tea she favored. Avery liked the way its subtle, calming scent filled the office. Together, many times, they'd explored Avery's tendency to rush ahead, to try to reach for solutions before she'd really begun to understand a problem—a characteristic that well served her military career, but wasn't always an asset in civilian life.

"For now, just the list, okay?" Dr. Santiago smiled, her eyes filled with warm humor. "Then, we go from there."

Avery nodded, agreeing to another exercise with what small portion of faith she could muster. She had a journal full of these little tasks, half-completed, and would try this one as well, but she'd done enough of them not to get her hopes up. She was fairly certain by now that writing in a journal like a teenage girl, pouring her feelings onto the page, wasn't going to fix her problems. Still, sometimes it helped to get things out of her head and down on paper, and even when it didn't, at least seeing her thoughts in black and white on a physical page often made them clearer.

"I come from a family of Southern farmers, doctor.

We don't have time for pain. If you break your arm, you still have to milk the cows."

"I know this well," Dr. Santiago replied, pointing a finger across her desk even as she jotted a few quick notes with the other hand. Avery appreciated that she never took notes during their sessions and each time only spent a few minutes doing so afterwards. Her focused attention when they spoke made an immense impact on how well Avery was able to connect with Dr. Santiago, to open up during their meetings for the sake of her own well-being.

"But you'll recall I've met your brother, Avery, on a day when he had to milk the cows—" she smiled, reaching across the desk to pat Avery's hand "—and I could see instantly that he loves you and wants to help you get to feeling better. Sometimes we have to teach the people around us how to care for us. They don't always know best." She set down her enameled pen and looked up, folding her hands on top of the notepad.

"Isaac is different," Avery said softly, without intending to. But when the doctor nodded, she continued. "He seems to know what I need, when I need it, without me having to tell him. He is kind and emotionally mature. And—"

She didn't think Dr. Santiago needed to know that just the sight of him made her heart run wild like an off-leash greyhound.

"He sounds wise and supportive, Avery." She paused, blinking. "I think this is a good thing, spending more time with him. Do you agree?"

"I think so," Avery said, hearing the waver in her own words.

Very little ever got past Dr. Santiago.

"But?"

"But—" Avery shifted, suddenly restless despite the couch's soft, inviting cushions "—even though he's wonderful, for some reason, I'm almost as afraid of him as I was of going off to a combat zone, and then of coming home," she admitted. Just saying the words out loud brought a little relief, but not enough.

When Avery stopped speaking, Dr. Santiago was silent for a few seconds. Avery liked that about her. The doctor didn't try to fill quiet with questions, but she also didn't hesitate to ask the often-difficult things that helped Avery get to the bottom of her fears. They had covered much ground together, but the thought of how much more there was to go made Avery feel suddenly fatigued even after the progress she'd made in their hour together.

"Well, let's talk this through, then," Dr. Santiago proposed, apparently ignoring or not overly concerned that their time was up. "What is it that you're afraid might happen?"

Avery considered the gently prodding question. If she'd learned anything about psychotherapy, it was that mining a heart was exhausting, painful, frustrating work that didn't yield overnight results. In the time that she'd been home, she'd only just scratched the surface of what she knew to be a vast iceberg, the largest portion of which remained hidden underwater. She'd come home thinking everything would be okay, but she quickly realized that although her military training covered extensive wartime coping mechanisms, she didn't know much of anything about returning to normal life.

Medication helped with her anxiety symptoms, at first, but it didn't help her forget the things she'd seen—the darkest corners of human behavior—and there were days she'd do just about anything to empty her mind of all she'd been exposed to. She wanted to believe that people were good, that they did the best they could with what they were given, but she wasn't so sure she bought that theory anymore.

"I guess I'm—"

The words to articulate her emotions wouldn't come, and a knot of frustration began to rise in her throat. Oh, how she hated to cry, especially in front of other people. She'd managed to get through years of providing medical care for battered soldiers without more than a few tears, but once she'd returned, it was as if all of those experiences joined to form a deluge, and there were days she couldn't keep her eyes dry.

"I think I'm afraid that it might be harder to let him all the way into my heart than it would be to shut him out."

Dr. Santiago took another sip of her tea, closing her eyes for a moment, thinking things over the way a friend would.

"What might happen if you show him the darkest parts of you, the places that scare you the most?" she asked, replacing her blue-and-white teacup in its saucer.

"I might—" Avery pulled in a breath as memories

slipped past floodgates "—I might love him someday. Maybe I already do. And then I might lose him."

Images of her best friend's face the last time she saw her, of the casual way, on the day Sophie died, that they'd traded shifts so Avery could care for her injured patient. Avery couldn't have predicted or stopped the downward spiral that resulted from a single wrong decision. On some level, she knew that. But it didn't change the fact that Sophie's son would grow up without his mother. It didn't change the fact that every time she ran into Sophie's husband—a circumstance she avoided more and more as much as she could—he would look at Avery and wonder why it was she who'd survived, and not his lovely, sweet wife.

Dr. Santiago must have understood the path Avery's thoughts had taken from the expression on her patient's face. She removed her hands from the teacup and folded them again across the notepad on her desk. Finally, she spoke quietly.

"That's very true," she said. "When we allow others to love us, and when we love them, there is always a price to pay, and paying that price is part of being human. We do it because none of us can be our best selves without others. None of us truly wants to be always alone."

It was Avery's turn to nod.

"But think of it this way, Avery." Dr. Santiago turned her hands, palms up. "If you really enjoy Isaac's company, if he brings you happiness and support, and all of the other wonderful things you've described—don't you think that you deserve those things?"

"No," Avery said, quickly. She didn't need to think about the answer to that question.

"I disagree," Dr. Santiago posed. "I'm sure Isaac has a choice in whom he spends time with. Why would he be spending so much time with you if you weren't also bringing him joy? Do you not deserve to take what he's offered in return?"

Avery didn't respond. Her heart was too full of aches and she was getting tired. They'd gotten to a place they couldn't surpass that day, or maybe ever, and suddenly, she just wanted to go home.

"Let's meet again next week, Avery. You've done so well today, and I know it's very hard on you." Dr. Santiago leaned over on her elbows, her forearms covering the large calendar that covered her desktop. "Listen. I want you to know how brave you are for coming in to see me, for keeping your appointments. The work you're doing here is difficult, but it's important, and you are doing an excellent job."

Avery felt that she was anything but brave. Bravery was what the soldiers she'd cared for had; it was in the sacrifices they'd made to serve their country in an effort to make the world a safer place. It wasn't sitting in a psychiatrist's office, talking about why she couldn't risk spending so much time with Isaac Meyer.

She picked up her shoulder bag and headed for the door.

Chapter Thirteen

The day of the 5K, Isaac stopped by Tommy's house to pick up Avery, pulling another box out of the back of his truck. But this time, it wasn't zucchini.

It was going to be a warm day. Already the sun was hot against his back as he headed toward the porch, Jane at his heels, but he didn't care. All he could see were hours and hours of time with Avery, hours he would fill doing his new favorite thing—making her as happy as humanly possible.

He rang the doorbell and Macy opened it with a big smile for him, getting flour all over his clothes as he stepped into her arms for a hug. "Oops," she said, attempting to wipe it off as Isaac laughed and batted her hands away so she couldn't just make things worse.

"Avery's in her room," she said, "I'll go get her for

you. Just head on into the kitchen and help yourself to a muffin."

Isaac stopped midstep. "There aren't any zucchini in them, are there?"

Macy winked at him over her shoulder. "Wouldn't you like to know?"

Armed with what he took to be a warning, he obeyed her anyway and found Tommy munching away on breakfast at the table.

"Isaac!" Tommy said, getting up to shake his hand. "Glad to see you, man." He offered Isaac a cup of coffee and brought one back, black, handing it across the table as he took his seat.

"It's good to see you, too."

"Sounds like you and Avery have become mighty close over the past few weeks," Tommy said, grinning over his World's Okayest Dad mug, which was made even funnier by the fact that Tommy was an inarguably excellent father.

"We have. And I'm glad you mentioned it because I want to talk to you about her."

Concern knitted Tommy's brows and Isaac waved his hand in the air to indicate that everything was okay.

"Nothing's wrong. Nothing at all. I just wanted to let you know that…that I'm in love with her. And that I have every intention of one day asking her to marry me."

Tommy beamed. "That's just wonderful! I'm so happy for both of you, and you absolutely have my blessing."

He looked over Isaac's shoulder and then lowered his voice.

"Just don't tell Macy. She'll go nuts and start planning things left and right before you even have a chance to pop the question. Trust me on that one."

Isaac laughed, happy to have told Avery's brother, his friend, and relieved that he'd reacted the way he had. "Oh, don't worry. I won't. And I'm not going to ask anytime soon."

He took a sip of his coffee, strong enough to add hair to his chest, just the way he liked it.

"Avery needs time. I want to make sure she's ready when I get to it and, anyway, people would think we were crazy if I asked her after less than a month."

Tommy narrowed his eyes. "Since when do you care what people think of you?"

Isaac grinned. "I don't. But Avery might. We're taking things slow, doing things right, building a solid foundation. We have all the time in the world."

Tommy nodded. "Have you told her how you feel, at least?"

Isaac shook his head. "I'm going to. Just haven't found the right moment yet."

"Well, when you do, I have no doubt you'll be pleased with the outcome." Tommy reached over and punched his friend in the shoulder. "That girl is head over heels, man. Head over heels. And I couldn't be happier that it's with my best friend."

"Morning, boys."

Isaac looked up at the sound of Avery's voice in the doorway, warm as butter. He practically jumped up from the table, eager to be near her, to touch her and to breathe in the sweet scent he'd missed overnight in her absence. They had agreed not to spend every night together, and he couldn't wait for the day when all he'd have to do was roll over in bed each morning and she'd be there, hair golden across her pillow in the morning light. He knew that he wanted to spend the rest of his life with her, and he hoped to God she felt the same.

He'd start to tell her that this morning.

Avery wrapped her arms around him, snuggling in close as he hugged her tight. "Good morning, sweetheart," he said into her hair. "How'd you sleep?"

"Like a baby." She looked up at him and her eyes were clear in the morning light peeking through the kitchen window. "Foggy's been good to me."

Her affection for the dog was evident in her voice, and Isaac thanked the stars that the two had made as good a fit as Hannah had thought they would. He made a note to do something special for Hannah as a thank-you.

"Where is the guy?"

"Oh, he's with the kids. They adore him."

Tommy chimed in. "It was a little tough getting them to understand what it means when his vest is on, but once we got that down, everybody's happy."

"Although they like him best off duty," Avery said, a grin brightening her already lovely face.

She wore a blue tank top that matched her eyes over another white one, and Isaac noted with pleasure that she'd already gained a couple of pounds. Skinny jeans hugged her perfectly curved bottom and he resisted the urge to put his hands all over her.

He always made sure their dates involved food, and even though Avery had called him out on it, she'd started to enjoy eating a little bit more, and they had a blast rediscovering her favorite meals.

"I've got something for you," Isaac said, taking Avery's hand to lead her out of the kitchen.

"See you kids later," Tommy called after them.

"What is it?" she asked, and Isaac laughed. Impatient—just like a kid at Christmas.

"You'll have to wait and see, now, won't you?"

He tugged her down the hallway and sat her down on the couch in the front sitting room, pulling the box he'd brought over to place at her feet. He'd taken a leap of faith on this one, and he hoped she'd like it.

"Open it," he said, and her eyes widened, pretty little crinkles at their corners as she smiled.

She picked up the box and pulled off the giant yellow bow, then made quick work of the soft green paper he'd chosen. Isaac couldn't remember when he'd last been so nervous. It wasn't like he was proposing now, yet the world seemed to hold its breath as he waited to see what she thought.

She pulled out each item, touching them softly, and as she realized what he'd done, her eyes filled with moisture.

"Oh, Isaac."

"I hope this is okay," he said, apprehensive.

On Thursday, after he'd picked her up from her therapy appointment, when Avery was busy with Foggy, he'd noticed a piece of paper on the ground in the room they'd been using at the training facility. Not wanting any of the dogs to get hold of it, he'd picked it up, intending to toss it into the recycling bin out back. But when he picked it up, the paper unfolded, and Isaac had seen what was written on it. It was a list, and he had everything on it memorized by now:

Things That Make Me Happy

Regency romance novels
The Beatles
Blue nail polish
80s movies
Homemade chocolate-chip cookies
Isaac Meyer
Foggy

He watched as she laid each object out on the floor— five of her very favorite Regency romances, he'd double-checked with Macy; every John Hughes film ever made; a few Beatles box-set albums; every shade of blue nail polish he could find; and a dozen chocolate-chip cookies, freshly baked in his kitchen that morning, using Nana's famous recipe—forming a circle around her.

When she was finished, she covered her mouth with a fist, and tears began to slide down her cheeks.

"I didn't mean to invade your privacy, Ave. I found the list on the ground at the training center, and, well… I couldn't help myself. I hope it's okay."

"Shut up, Isaac," she said, crawling out of her circle

of happiness and into his lap, covering his face with kisses as he laughed, thankful he hadn't screwed up.

Finally she stilled, looking into his eyes. "You know, I don't have any of this stuff. When I left for the military, I pretty much got rid of everything, and when I got back, I never got around to buying any of the things I enjoy. I guess I wasn't sure if I would stay."

He brushed hair back from her eyes and kissed her, long and slow, on her sweet mouth.

"Please do," he said. "Please stay."

"I plan to," she said. "Now that I have you."

He smiled, leaning his forehead against hers.

"Thank you, Isaac," she whispered. "Thank you. For everything."

Later that morning, they all piled into two trucks and drove to Peach Leaf Park, where the local animal shelter's 5K fund-raiser was scheduled to take place.

Avery and Isaac unloaded Foggy and Jane, snapping on their harnesses and leashes and Foggy's vest, ready to practice being in public in a place chock-full of every kind of distraction available.

A banner welcomed them as they entered the park, Tommy, Macy and the kids trailing along behind. The air was thick with the smell of delicious food: hot dogs, funnel cake and popcorn, all ready to reward the serious racers after a day's run, Isaac joked.

Avery definitely planned to sample everything, glad that her favorite jeans were close to fitting again, proud of the feminine curves that had begun to make their reappearance. Most women would be horrified to gain five pounds in a few weeks, she mused, but she needed the weight, and Dr. Santiago would be thrilled at her progress. Avery definitely was.

Isaac made everything better, even food.

She made no effort to hide the fact that she was checking him out as they walked. He looked great in a soft, dark green T-shirt that hugged the muscles underneath, and khaki cargo shorts. His unruly hair—hair she'd had plenty of chances to bury her fingers in—just touched his collar under an ancient Peach Leaf Panthers baseball cap.

Her hand felt right at home in his as they walked, a dog on either side, and for the moment, Avery couldn't imagine how her life could be any more perfect, or any different from what it had been a few weeks ago.

She hadn't even known what she wanted until it landed right in front of her. Now she would do anything to keep it, to keep him.

Isaac. *Her* Isaac.

They strolled around the park for a while, checking out all the booths and making sure Foggy and Jane had plenty of water before they set off to walk the three-plus miles. Isaac told Avery that the race organizers, being animal folks, of course, had opted to start the race by shouting into a megaphone, rather than using the customary air horn or gunshot.

Finally, they gathered at the starting line, waving at Tommy, Macy and the kids, who were going to cheer them on from the sidelines. When the announcer gave the go, Isaac and Avery set off at a quick pace, Foggy and Jane trotting just ahead.

They'd spent a couple of hours that week working with Foggy on Isaac's idea of keeping people at a safe distance from her with the block command, and he showed off his training with honor that day, making sure to keep in front of Avery so that she didn't get too close to anyone, and the crowd, overwhelming at first, lessened its effect on her after a time. She relaxed into her footsteps, keeping a steady pace, enjoying the late spring sunshine on her face, the gentle breeze in her hair and the cool, dewy morning air.

Occasionally, as they walked, Isaac looked over to check on her, and they stopped every once in a while to give the dogs water in a little travel bowl.

The four of them together felt…like family, and Avery let every minute of it soak into her soul, replacing bad memories with good ones. If she spent enough time with Isaac, she knew, the happy would begin to outweigh the sad. It was only a matter of time.

At the finish line, Sylvia and Ben greeted them with fresh water bottles, and they accepted the paw-shaped medals the race officials draped over their necks for completing the distance.

They were headed toward the food booths when Avery thought she heard someone calling her name. Isaac turned as she did and she saw Nathan coming toward them, Connor hurrying to keep pace, his little hand in his father's.

"Avery," Nathan said, breathing hard. He stopped a few feet away and lifted Connor into his arms. "If you've got a minute, I'd love to talk to you. That is—"

he glanced from her to Isaac and back again "—if that's okay with you."

She swallowed, her throat tight, and Foggy must have picked up on her nervousness because he stepped forward and sat down between her and Nathan, calmly but with obvious confidence. He didn't even need the block command; he would protect his girl if he needed to without being asked. He would make sure nothing got to her that might cause her to be afraid or upset.

Her heartbeat slowed to normal, knowing her furry companion was there. She lowered a hand and placed it on his neck, letting Foggy know she was okay, and that she appreciated his gesture.

"Yes, that would be all right with me," she said, her voice sounding stronger than she'd anticipated. She looked to Isaac, whose hand had come to rest on her shoulder, reassuring her that he was there for her, as well. Her two guys, there to keep her safe. "I'll be right back, Isaac."

"We'll be right here," he said, taking Foggy's leash as she handed it over. The dog wasn't too happy about having her leave him behind, but he calmly cooperated and followed Isaac and Jane to a nearby drink stand.

She and Nathan walked over to a picnic table and sat down across from each other. Nathan put Connor down next to him and handed his son a fire truck from his backpack.

It must be his favorite toy, Avery thought, as she recalled seeing it the other day.

"Avery," Nathan said, his voice full of emotion. He looked down at the table and she could see that whatever he was about to say was taking a lot of his courage to get out.

"I'm surprised you want to talk to me after the other day," she said.

"I know, and, Avery, I'm so sorry about what happened then. I didn't mean to act like that. I was a real jerk and I wish I could take it back."

"No, Nathan. I'm the one that's sorry. I shouldn't have pushed myself on you like that. It wasn't fair after all you've been through. I was being selfish as hell and I want you to know I didn't mean to bring all that back for you."

He was quiet for a long moment and Avery sensed that he was getting his bearings, that he was trying to hold on to his emotion so it didn't break free and embarrass them both. She wanted to tell him that he would feel better if he just let it go, that it only hurt to keep it inside, as she'd only recently begun to learn, thanks to Isaac's presence and support in her life.

If everyone had their own equivalent of an Isaac and a Foggy, she thought, *the world would be a better place*.

"I miss her so damn much, Avery. Sometimes I can't stand it. Sometimes I think I can't go on because of how much it hurts to do all this without her." He put his face in his hands and glanced over at Connor as if worried that his son might hear, but the child continued to play happily with his truck, lost in his own safe, peaceful world.

"But you have to, don't you, Nathan?" she said firmly, giving Nathan some of the courage she'd gained from Isaac. "You have to keep going for Connor. He needs you. Sophie trusted you to take care of him if something happened to her, and she would want you to be strong." She offered him a weak smile as he swiped his hands over his face and met her eyes.

"Yeah, she would, wouldn't she?" he said, his eyes softening at her memory.

"She was so strong," Avery said. "She was the bravest, best woman I've ever known, and I wish I had her back. I miss my best friend, and I know you miss your wife, but she wouldn't have been too happy if she'd seen the hot messes we've turned out to be."

Nathan laughed, a tight, sharp sound that hinted at the extent of his sorrow.

"I lost a friend," she said, her voice quiet, "but you lost your wife, and I can't even begin to imagine how hard that must be for you."

He closed his eyes.

"But that doesn't give me the right to shut you out, or to keep you from seeing Connor. Sophie would have hated that I've done that for so long."

Shame filled his face, and Avery wanted to tell him that he'd done nothing wrong, that grief was almost impossible to bear sometimes, and other times, it could only barely be tolerated.

He looked over at Connor. "The only reason I've done so is because it was too hard for me, but seeing you the other day…it brought back too many memories of all the good times the three of us had when she was alive, before you both left. I realized how much I've been shielding him from because of my own pain.

And that's not fair. I owe it to my son to be the best father I can be, and I know now that I wasn't doing that."

He looked up at the sky as if deciding whether or not to say more.

"Did you know I don't even have photographs of her in our home? I put them all away when she died." His voice wavered. "I just couldn't bear to look at her, you know?"

His eyes were rimmed with red as he reached over and took Avery's hand.

"That's in the past now. I took them all out the day we saw you in the park, and I've been showing them to Connor every day, so that I can teach him how wonderful his mama was."

Avery felt tears prickle at the back of her eyes.

"And I'm sorry, Avery. I want you to know that I don't blame you for what happened to my wife. She was stubborn, and what she wanted, she got. And she was an amazing woman who wanted to serve her country almost as much as she wanted to be a mom. It was important to her to do her duty, and it was important to her to go with you. She loved you so much, you know. I think she would have followed you anywhere."

They both laughed at the truth of his statement and Avery choked up, wiping away a few drops that had fallen from her eyes.

"I want you to know that you can see Connor anytime you want. You are always welcome in our home, as are Isaac and your dogs." Nathan smiled at Connor. "I'm sure this little guy would love to have them over for a playdate sometime. In the near future, Avery, you hear?"

"Of course." She squeezed his hand. "Thank you, Nathan. I didn't know how much I needed to hear those things until now. I promise I won't be a stranger."

He nodded, and they were both quiet, realizing they had broken frozen ground and could now sow seeds that would become their futures. They could make choices for themselves now, rather than holding on to the grief that had rendered them immobile for so long.

"You know," Avery said, speaking almost as much to herself as she was to Nathan, "when I joined the military, I knew the risks and the danger, and even though there was always a little fear, I felt prepared."

Nathan nodded as his eyes filled, and she continued.

"I knew exactly what I was getting into—" she swallowed "—but I had no idea how to get out. They don't tell you how hard it's going to be to get back to a normal life, if that's ever even possible."

Nathan squeezed her hand. They didn't need to say any more about it.

When Connor grew bored with his fire truck, Nathan reminded him who Avery was, and the two of them chatted for a long time about preschool and when would she please come over and bring her puppies to see him.

Avery's heart was loads lighter when they parted ways and she returned to Isaac's side. He handed her a fresh-squeezed lemonade from a nearby stand and gave her back Foggy's leash.

"Everything okay with Nathan?" Isaac asked, his

brown eyes full of worry as he studied her face for clues about how their visit had gone.

"Better than ever," she said. "We're okay now." She took a sip of the drink, sweetness and tartness teasing her taste buds at the same time.

"So glad to hear it, sweetie."

"We'll have to bring Jane and Foggy by to meet Connor sometime. He's super excited about being around dogs. Nathan works full-time and Connor goes to preschool, so they can't have one of their own right now. It would mean a lot to them if he could play with ours."

"Consider it done," Isaac said, smiling. "He seems like a sweet kid."

"He is, just like his mom was."

"Do you want one someday?" Isaac asked. "Kids, I mean."

Avery looked up at him, surprised. "Isaac Meyer," she teased. "Are you asking me if I'll have your children someday?"

He gave her his sexiest grin, tilting his head so that his dark hair grazed his shoulder, looking for all the world like a rake from one of her favorite books.

"Would that be a problem?" he asked.

"Actually, no," she said, pushing her chin forward to show him she wasn't intimidated by his suggestion of commitment. "And yes, I do want kids. Someday."

Isaac's expression showed her he wasn't satisfied with her answer.

She took another sip of lemonade, drawing it out to bug him.

"My kids?" he asked.

"Yes, idiot," she said, reaching across the table to poke his chest. "Your kids."

They were both being silly, mostly, but now they were dead serious as they caught each other's eye.

It was in that second that Avery knew precisely how she felt about Isaac Meyer—there was no longer any question—and exactly how to articulate it.

The words were on the tip of her tongue when she heard the first blast. Lemonade spilled across the table as she knocked it over in her hurry to get cover. She flew under the picnic table and huddled there, her arms wrapped over her knees, head down as a few more explosions erupted and, once again, the world went black around her.

Chapter Fourteen

Isaac rushed to Avery's side where she crouched under the table, but Foggy made it to her first. He was licking her face between sharp barks, doing his best to get his body as close to hers as possible, but it wasn't helping.

She shook violently, her skin pale and cold like marble, and her hands whipped at him when he tried to touch her. Finally, he was able to get her into his arms, where he held her for several minutes until the rapid heaving of her chest began to subside. He lifted her up and lay her down in the grass underneath the picnic table. Foggy draped himself over her torso, waiting patiently for her to get back to normal.

Isaac knew she kept antianxiety medication at home, but she'd told him she didn't need to bring it with her, that she was okay without it almost all of the time.

Now he cursed himself for not insisting that she bring it along, just in case; he wouldn't make that mistake again.

But as he watched, Foggy began to lick her face again, and eventually her eyes lost their glaze, their iciness returning to their calm, ocean-water appearance. She noticed the dog and wrapped her arms around him, pulling him close as he continued to wash her with kisses.

Foggy worked almost as fast as medication, without the unpleasant side effects that sometimes accompanied drugs.

Isaac's heart nearly burst as he watched the dog take care of his person, and a thought hit him like a bullet to the chest.

If only Stephen had waited. If only he'd stuck around for just a few more years until Isaac started this business. If only he hadn't left before Isaac got a chance to save him.

As Avery looked into his eyes, he felt anger flood through him like hot blood, misplaced rage at his inability to keep Stephen from taking his own life, and instead of doing what he should have, instead of comforting her and making sure that she was okay after what she'd perceived as trauma, he took that out on her.

He grasped her forearms and forced her to look at him. Her eyes were full of fear, *of him*. He hated himself for that, but couldn't stop once he'd started. All the things he'd never been able to say, all that he'd never been able to express to his brother, who'd selfishly left him here to take care of their mom, to fend for himself without a father.

"You can't do this to me, Avery. You can't leave me like that. It scares the crud out of me to think I've lost you when you disappear on me that way."

She stared at him, confusion etched into her features now, her eyes huge. "It's okay, Isaac. I'm fine. I just heard the fireworks and got startled, but look, I'm okay." She held out her arms for him to see. "Foggy helped me and my episode lasted only a few minutes. Everything's fine. Really."

"No, Avery. It's not fine," he shouted. He didn't know what was happening to him but he couldn't keep his voice down. "They should know better than to allow fireworks at something like this, where there are animals everywhere anyway, but you can't do that to me— you can't scare me like that. I thought I'd lost you."

His head spun as he fought desperately to make sense of the confusing flood of emotions darting through his brain and heart.

"What's the matter with you, Isaac?" she asked, and he caught the hurt in her voice. He knew he should apologize, but somehow he couldn't form the words.

What *was* the matter with him? This wasn't Stephen. He knew that. At least part of him did, but another part…another part wasn't able to separate the two. He'd loved his brother, yet he'd been unable to save him. No matter how much he'd wanted to, he'd never been able to heal that dark space inside of Stephen. And now… now he wondered if he would ever be able to do that for Avery.

If he cared for her as much as he knew he did, would he always wonder about the possibility of danger, of her

PTSD taking over, of the darkness winning? Would he live his life afraid of losing her?

A small voice inside said *yes*. Yes, he would. And as much as it had hurt to lose his brother—losing Avery would somehow be worse. Losing Avery, he knew suddenly, would destroy him.

"I see," she said, her features resigned. She looked... shattered. "Look, Isaac. I laid everything out on the table when we met. You know that I have some pretty big problems—they were never a secret. Because of the way we met, I never even got a chance to decide if I wanted them to be, not that I would have been able to hide them for long. But if you can't handle being around me, if you're going to freak out like this whenever something happens to me, well...I can't. I just can't do this."

She crawled out from under the table as he watched, frozen in place, powerless to stop her. It was too late when he came to his senses, when he finally understood that the reason he'd lashed out was the very reason he absolutely needed her to stay.

"Avery," he called after her as she grabbed Foggy's leash and started jogging away without looking back, leaving him and Jane there in the dirt. "Avery, wait!"

But it wasn't enough. She was gone, and it was his fault.

Avery had no idea where she was headed. She just ran and ran, poor Foggy jogging along beside her.

She finally stopped when she reached the duck pond. She sat on the rock bench to catch her breath and pulled Foggy's portable dish out of her pocket, pouring water from her bottle into the little bowl and setting it down. Foggy lapped it up quickly and she gave him more until he was no longer thirsty.

Tears came, fast and hot, but no matter how many times she went over the scene in her head, she couldn't figure out what had happened to Isaac back there. What on earth had made him so blistering mad at her? He'd been so out of character, yelling at her like that, and it scared her. She hadn't understood him when he'd tried to explain why he was so upset; none of what he'd said had made sense. What was that he'd said about losing her? He wasn't going to lose her. She was right freaking *there*. And she'd given him more of herself than she'd shared with anyone in as long as she could remember.

She shook her head and pulled in deep breaths, going over the previous moments until her temples began to throb. She had no idea how long she sat there like that, staring into the water, right at the same spot that Isaac had first kissed her.

Everything had been so perfect.

What had she done to make it so wrong?

"Avery."

His voice behind her back caused the hair on her neck to stand. She was mad at him, but still her body reacted viscerally to his nearness as he came into view, sitting beside her on the rock as Jane wandered over to stare at the ducks.

A long silence passed before he spoke.

"Avery, please forgive me. I don't know what got into me back there."

"Well, that makes two of us, then," she said, her voice sad and bitter.

They sat in silence until he cleared his throat.

"Just tell me this."

She turned to look at him.

"Are you okay?"

His eyes were full of agony, and she wanted to touch him. But she wasn't sure if that was the right thing to do. He'd been so angry at her for no real reason, and it had challenged her trust in him.

"Yes, I'm okay. Are you?"

"I think so," he said, his voice pleading. "Avery, I'm so very sorry."

"What was that, Isaac? What happened? Why did you blow up like that on me? I hate that you shouted at me that way."

He shut his eyes tight at her words.

"I was taking something out on you that had nothing to do with you."

"I don't think I understand."

"I was the one who found Stephen," he said, barely able to hear his own words. "I was the one who found him after he died, and it nearly killed me. I think a part of me sees you as being fragile, like he was. And if you don't get better, the same thing might happen to you."

She put her hand on his forearm and her touch warmed his skin.

"Oh, Isaac," she said. "I'm not Stephen. I'm not going to hurt myself. I've got so much to stick around for. I've got you and Foggy and my family. I'm not going anywhere. Not if I can help it."

"I'm so sorry I lashed out at you like that, but I can't lose you. I just can't."

"I do worry, though, sometimes. It's just that…well…I worry that I might not ever get completely better. What if I always have these involuntary responses to things, and I'm never all the way back to normal? What if I can't ever hold down a job again? What if I'm a danger to you, or—" she swallowed "—to…to a child?"

"You'll lean on me," he said. "Whatever happens, you and I will handle it together. You won't have to be alone anymore, not if you don't want to."

She thought about what he'd said, wanting desperately to tell him that everything was okay, that they should just forget about it. But she knew that wasn't entirely true. Everything wasn't okay, and if she was going to start a relationship with this man, to maybe start on a path to building a life with him, then she needed everything to be out in the open. She wanted everything this time—no secrets, no holding back. She knew there would always be things to be afraid of. Just like him, she was afraid of losing something precious to her, but somehow she knew they were both ready to take that risk.

If the past few weeks had taught her anything, it was that some things were worth being afraid for. And he was worth it.

"Look, Isaac, I want to forgive you, and I want us to get past this, but if we're going to do that, we have to be honest with one another."

His eyes met hers and the threat of fresh tears choked her next words.

"I need you to know that I'm not your brother. I'm not going to end my life." She offered him a sad smile. "I have too much good to even think about taking that path out. But at the same time, I can't have you treating me like I'm another project. I know you love working with people with PTSD, but somehow you have to find a way to separate me from your work. I refuse to live my life wondering if you're just using me to atone for what you *think* of as your failure to save your brother."

He nodded, slowly, and stayed silent for a long moment.

"You're right about that, Avery. I didn't see it before, but I think I may have thought of you that way at first."

He reached over to grasp her hands, threading their fingers together, sending sparks through her.

"But I don't any longer. I understand that now. In just a short time, you've become everything to me, and I think I worried that I might lose you just as fast. I placed the weight of Stephen's choice on you, and that wasn't fair. I see now that you're your own woman, with your own life to live, and I know now that you're far stronger than Stephen ever was."

She swallowed, working to hold back an onslaught of relieved tears.

"I don't see you as a project—I see you as a partner. Someone I want to share my world with. I think it took this situation for me to truly understand that, and I'm so very sorry that I lashed out at you. I didn't know what to do with this new knowledge, with the realization of how much I care for you, but I do now. I want to continue helping you to train Foggy, but I also want much, much more. I will make you my world, if you let me."

As she looked into his eyes, she knew he meant every single word he said. In just the past few weeks, her life had changed completely, for the better, and Isaac was at the center of those changes.

She knew he couldn't *fix* her, and she didn't need him to. She would do the work herself, and she would be the victor over her own struggles. But he was right—they could be partners. They could share their pain and joy; they could encourage each other through the worst of it and laugh together through the best. She wanted that as much as he did.

"I'm in. But only if I can convince you that you're not going to lose me, Isaac. I promise you that. I'm here for good." She tickled his chin with her fingers, then pulled it so that he would look into her eyes. "Whether you want me or not."

Now was the time they'd both been waiting for. Now was the time to tell him how she felt.

"I do. I do want you." He swallowed, putting his hands on her face. "I love you, Avery Abbott. And I always will."

Her blue eyes filled, spilling over when she closed them. When they opened again, they were overflowing with joy, with peace.

"I love you, too, Isaac Meyer."

As they made their way back to the chaos of booths and families and food, hand in hand, a man dressed in a navy blue polo shirt and slacks—a bit formal for a

5K on a warm spring day—approached and stopped in front of them, holding out a hand.

"Are you Mr. Isaac Meyer?" he asked.

"I am," Isaac said, shaking the man's offered hand. "What can I do for you, sir?"

"Quite a bit, I hope," the man said, giving a little laugh.

Isaac smiled tentatively, uncertain what was so darn funny.

"Mr. Meyer, I'm Fred Palmer," the man said, continuing when Isaac stared back at him with a blank expression. "Fred Palmer," he said again, "of Palmer Motors."

"Oh, yes," Isaac said, the pieces clicking into place. "I didn't recognize you, sir. You look a little different from your TV commercials.

Mr. Palmer laughed again and Isaac decided he liked this guy.

"As well you shouldn't. The wife's had me on a diet the past few months and I've lost about thirty pounds, but they needed to go."

"Well, then, congratulations are in order," Avery chimed in.

Isaac apologized for not introducing them and was quick to remedy that.

"Mr. Palmer," he said, "This is Avery Abbott." He turned to Avery, who stood near his side, holding Foggy's and Jane's leashes, and his heart nearly burst through his chest at the sight of her beautiful face. "My girlfriend."

She beamed at him before he turned back to Mr. Palmer.

"Pleased to meet you, Ms. Abbott," the older gentleman said. "I knew your father—we went to school together at Peach Leaf High, ages ago. And, may I say, thank you for your service."

Avery lowered her chin a little, nodding in gratitude.

He turned back to Isaac.

"Mr. Meyer, let's get right down to business. I have a proposal I'd like to make."

"Of course, sir, I'd love to hear it. What's on your mind?"

A broad smile spread across the man's face, lifting his plump cheeks.

"Well, son, if I do say so myself, my company's doing pretty good, and when that's the case, I like to show my thanks to the community in some way. I wouldn't have the business that I do if it wasn't for the great folks in this town."

"That's very generous of you, Mr. Palmer. I know Peach Leaf owes a lot to you."

The older man waved a hand. "It owes me nothing, son. I was born and raised here and I run a solid company. It's in my power to give back and it's something I enjoy doing, but that's beside the point."

Isaac was beginning to realize where this was going and he couldn't help the excited energy that sprinted up his spine. Mr. Palmer was known for his donations to local causes, and if what he'd heard about the man was even half-true, he could help a lot of people in the near future.

"The point is, son, I've been watching you for a long time, and you're doing some amazing work with vets and rescue dogs, and, well, I've got a soft spot for them—" he glanced in Avery's direction "—for you."

Isaac nodded, his palms sweaty.

"So, here it is. If it's all right with you, I'd like to make a donation, Mr. Meyer."

Isaac stifled a laugh. "Of course it's all right with me."

Avery squeezed his hand.

"In the amount of half a million dollars."

"Holy cow!" Avery bounced up and down with the energy of a happy child and Isaac couldn't help but do the same right along with her before smothering their generous donor with a thousand thank-yous.

"No need to thank me, son," Mr. Palmer said gruffly before moving on, but Isaac caught the shimmer at the corner of the old man's eye.

"I'd like you to use it to sponsor as many veterans as you can, as long as you keep taking and training dogs from the local shelter. You've got a gift for it, Meyer, and I've seen how much you've helped the ones who serve our country—especially my own boy."

Isaac recalled training with Gary Palmer and his Lab, Tex, a few months back. Gary had lost his legs to a mine and was wheelchair bound. Tex had given Gary his smile back, not to mention helping him perform daily tasks with a lot more ease.

"Thank you, again, Mr. Palmer, but Gary and Tex did all the work."

Mr. Palmer chuckled and Isaac nearly choked, overwhelmed at the amount of money the man had just given his organization.

"Truly. I can't thank you enough. You're helping a lot of folks, Mr. Palmer."

"You are, Isaac. You are," Mr. Palmer corrected.

The old man shook Isaac's hand again and bid them good day, promising to be in touch with the details of the donation the following Monday.

As soon as he walked away, Avery threw herself into Isaac's arms and peppered his face with kisses. He twirled her around and around, causing Foggy and Jane to bark at their outburst of glee.

"Oh. My. Goodness," Avery screamed. "Can you believe it? Half a million dollars? Half a million bucks, Isaac. Can you imagine how many people that will help?"

Isaac burst out laughing. "I can, actually," he said. "I'm doing the math in my head right now, and it's… epic."

He stopped spinning and set Avery's feet back on the ground, kissing her nose. She was absolutely beautiful in the afternoon light, sunshine glinting off her golden hair, her blue eyes sparkling with delight. Her happiness, new and precious and hard-earned, was contagious. This joyful Avery was the most magnificent thing he'd ever seen.

He pulled her close so she could see his face.

"But with that much financial backing, I'll need more help, you know?"

"Of course. You'll have to hire more trainers and have people to help you find dogs at the shelter, and—"

"And, I want you," he said.

"Me? What do you mean?"

"I mean, I want you to join me. I'm going to promote Hannah to manager, and I want you to be my new assistant."

Avery's face lit up when she got what he was saying.

"Are you serious?"

"As a heart attack."

"But I have no training. I'm a nurse, not a dog trainer."

"But you have what it takes to make a great one. You're a natural with Fogs and you'll be amazing once you're certified. Besides," Isaac said, grabbing her hand to lead her back to Tommy and Macy, "we have plenty to fund your classes now, don't we?"

"I would say so," she answered, giggling.

"I've had you with me for almost a month now, and it has been, without contest, the best almost-month of my life. I'm not about to let you go now, Avery."

He stopped to kiss her long and hard, right there in the middle of the park. When they caught their breaths, Avery gave him a big smile, her face flushed from sunshine and the sensation of his lips on hers.

"Well, that's good news," she said, "Because I wasn't lying when I told you I'm not planning on going anywhere. And pretty soon, I'm going to need a new job."

"You've got one," Isaac said, pulling her close. "As long as you want."

"How about forever?" she asked, the question holding far more weight than what her words had indicated.

"Forever isn't long enough," he answered.

"Are you happy, Isaac Meyer?"

"The happiest," he said. "Because of you."

Epilogue

July Fourth, one year later

Morning light slipped in through the blinds of Isaac and Avery's bedroom window, spreading golden rays across her blond hair.

He watched her sleep, humbled by the simple rise and fall of her chest as she inhaled and exhaled in perfect rhythm, wondering again where he'd gone so right—how he'd become the lucky man who got to wake up next to such a beautiful, amazing woman each morning.

Isaac leaned over to kiss her forehead, glad when her lips curved to smile at him. Slipping out of bed, he tucked the sheets around her shoulders and roused the dogs from where they slept, tangled together on the window seat.

The three of them went downstairs and Isaac opened the back door to let Foggy and Jane out, turning on the coffeepot. As it sputtered to life, starting up the strong brew he preferred, he walked into the dining room where he kept a small desk for business when he wasn't at the training facility. Grinning, he pulled out the office chair and sat, reaching into the bottom drawer, all the way to the very back.

He stopped when his fingers touched cool velvet, and pulled out a small box, lifting the lid. It still took his breath away every time he looked at this symbol of his love for her.

The past year of his life had been wonderful beyond words. Avery had passed her dog training certification exam with flying colors, and she and Foggy were an incredible team. Watching the two of them work together to help other veterans and dogs form partnerships brought him more happiness, more fulfillment, than anything he'd ever witnessed before in all the years he'd owned the facility. And to him, she was a greater partner than he ever could have hoped for.

Of course they had their tough days; of course things weren't perfect, but that didn't matter. What mattered, he had come to understand, was that they were together through the ups and downs. She was there for him, truly understood him when the ache of missing Stephen was too much to bear. And he did his very best to be a source of strength for her when she had nightmares and the—thankfully rare, now—panic attacks that still scared her so badly.

Each time he glimpsed the simple, elegant ring, he

grew more and more excited about this day—a day he'd anticipated for so long now.

And today—the big day—was no different. He couldn't wait any longer; it was time.

Grabbing a piece of string and snapping shut the lid, Isaac headed back to the kitchen and poured a cup of coffee for himself, leaving it black, then one for Avery, stirring in the ample amount of cream and sugar that his girl liked so much.

He set the cups on the kitchen counter and opened the back door, letting the dogs back in.

"All right, Foggy. You ready for your big job?"

The dog sat and raised his paw, giving Isaac a high five.

"Okay, then," he said. "Good deal. Let's get you all set."

He knelt down, pulled the ring out of his pocket and made a loop through its band with the piece of string, then tied it to Foggy's collar.

"This is it, boy," he said. "Have you got my back?"

Foggy barked.

"Shhh! We don't want to wake Mom just yet, okay?"

Back in the kitchen, he picked up the coffees, padding back upstairs as quietly as he could with two rambunctious dogs in tow.

When he reached the landing, Isaac took a deep breath, not because he had doubts, but because he could hardly contain the joy that threatened to burst out from under his skin.

That is, if she said yes.

He had to remind himself that there were two possible outcomes, though only one was worth dwelling on.

Avery woke to kisses, lots and lots of wet kisses.

"Foggy!" she chided. "I wasn't having a nightmare, boy."

She laughed and opened her eyes.

"What has gotten into you?" She tried to push the dog away, but he wasn't having it. Foggy jumped up onto the bed and lay down, paws on her chest.

"Morning," Isaac said, coming into the room, holding two cups of coffee. He kissed her forehead and put Avery's cup on her nightstand, then walked back to his side of the bed and slid under the covers.

"I think Foggy's trying to tell you something."

Isaac had a funny look on his face—overwhelmed, but happy—as if he anticipated something good, like a little boy on Christmas.

Avery didn't give it a second thought. He always looked like that since she'd moved in, a fact that made her smile every time she thought of it.

She rubbed her eyes and looked at the clock on her bedside table, groaning when she saw the hour.

"You guys are up way too early."

Isaac just grinned and took a sip of his coffee. He set the cup down and snuggled in closer.

"Foggy," he said, "roll over."

"What are you goofs up to?"

Foggy obeyed and flipped over to show off his tummy, making Avery laugh.

"I see you've learned a new trick, boy. Is that what you guys have been doing so early this morning?"

She gave his tummy an obligatory scratch, then rubbed under his chin. Something cold and metallic tapped against her fingers.

"What's this, Foggy?" she asked, tugging it out from the folds of his fur, gasping when it finally dawned on her what she held in her hand. Her pulse drummed at her temples, blocking out all sound.

"Oh, my gosh," she cried, a hand flying to her mouth as tears brimmed at the edges of her lids. "Isaac. It's just beautiful."

She gripped the ring and, with shaking hands, untied the string that attached it to Foggy's collar. Pulling in a breath, her eyes surveyed her surroundings, soaking in everything so she could remember it every day for the rest of her life.

A life she would spend with Isaac, a man she'd grown to love more than she ever thought possible.

He lifted the ring from her palm and got out of the bed, moving to kneel at her side.

"Avery Abbott. Will you marry me?"

She nodded, unable to say anything for a moment as tears rolled down her cheeks. Then, finally, it came—the word that would seal them together forever.

A word she'd said many times over the past year.

To new friends, to a job as a trainer that she absolutely adored, to events and places and things she'd never dreamed she would be able to experience.

And now to the man she loved more than anything else in the world.

"Yes," she said. "Yes, Isaac. I absolutely will marry you."

He slid the ring on her finger, then jumped up from the floor and right into the bed, covering her in kisses, wrapping his arms around her as she laughed, and cried, and laughed some more.

* * * * *

REQUEST YOUR FREE BOOKS!
2 FREE NOVELS PLUS 2 FREE GIFTS!

H HARLEQUIN®

SPECIAL EDITION

Life, Love & Family

HSE15

Joaquin nodded. "It was interesting. I saw a side of your father I'd never seen before. I have acquired a brand-new appreciation for him."

"That makes me so happy. You don't even know. I wish everyone could see him the way you do."

"Thanks for having him invite me."

Zoe held up her hand. "Actually, all I did was ask him if you were coming tonight, and he's the one who decided to invite you. He really likes you, Joaquin. And so do I."

He was silent for a moment, just looking at her in a way that she couldn't read. For a second, she was afraid he was going to friend-zone her again.

"I like you, too, Zoe. You know what I like most about you?"

She shook her head.

"You always see the best in everyone, even in me. I know I haven't been the easiest person to get to know."

Zoe laughed. Even if he was hard to get to know, Joaquin obviously had no idea what a great guy he was.

"I wish I could claim that as a heroic quality," she said. "But it's not hard to see the good in you. I mean, good grief, half the women in the office are in love with you."

He made a face that said he didn't believe her.

"But I don't want to share you."

He answered her by lowering his head and covering her mouth with his. It was a kiss that she felt all the way down to her curled toes.

When they finally came up for air, he said, "In case you're wondering, I just made a move on you."

Don't miss
FORTUNE'S PRINCE CHARMING
by Nancy Robards Thompson,
available May 2016 wherever
Harlequin® Special Edition books and ebooks are sold.

www.Harlequin.com

JUST CAN'T GET ENOUGH?

Join our social communities
and talk to us online.

You will have access to the latest
news on upcoming titles and special
promotions, but most importantly,
you can talk to other fans about your
favorite Harlequin reads.

Harlequin.com/Community

Facebook.com/HarlequinBooks

Twitter.com/HarlequinBooks

Pinterest.com/HarlequinBooks

Love the Harlequin book you just read?

Your opinion matters.

Review this book on your favorite book site, review site, blog or your own social media properties and share your opinion with other readers!

THE WORLD IS BETTER WITH

Romance

Harlequin has everything from contemporary, passionate and heartwarming to suspenseful and inspirational stories.

Whatever your mood,
we have a romance just for you!

Connect with us to find your next great read, special offers and more.

f /HarlequinBooks

🐦 @HarlequinBooks

www.HarlequinBlog.com

www.Harlequin.com/Newsletters

◆HARLEQUIN®

A *Romance* FOR EVERY MOOD™

www.Harlequin.com

Dear Reader,

I love every single book I've written, each for a different reason. But I'm learning as an author that some books are just extra special. *An Officer and Her Gentleman* is absolutely one of those books for me.

I've never served in the military and I've never seen combat, but almost every single one of us has known at least one person affected by war and its aftermath. Many of us can't even begin to understand what it would be like to be in battle ourselves, or to lose someone to such violence—and physical scars are only part of it. So many of our brave women and men come home from war with invisible wounds, and it isn't always easy to understand how to help them manage their pain. With Avery Abbott, I've done my very best to explore just one of the many ways we have of helping soldiers adjust back to civilian life when they come home changed.

I am not an expert, but the field of animal therapy is one of the most fascinating things in the world to me, and the possibilities that animals hold for healing humans seem almost endless. I hope you enjoy watching Avery, Isaac, and a special dog named Foggy fall in love and work to heal broken hearts as much as I enjoyed writing their story.

And it is my sincere hope, if you or a loved one has ever suffered physical or emotional scars of any kind, that you are able to someday find peace.

Very best,

Amy Woods